SUNRISE to SUNSET

An Anthology of Summer Reading

CHARLOTTE COLE, EDITOR

First published by The Women's Press Ltd, 1997
A member of the Namara Group
34 Great Sutton Street, London EC1V 0DX

British Library Cataloguing-in-Publication Data
A catalogue record for this book is available from the British Library

ISBN 0 7043 4536 6

Phototypeset in 9½/12pt Goudy Old Style by Intype London Ltd
Printed and bound in Great Britain by Caledonian International

··
PERMISSIONS

The Women's Press would like to thank the following:

Bonnie Burnard, care of Felicity Bryan, for permission to reprint 'Grizzly Mountain' from *Women of Influence*, 1993.

Jonathan Cape for permission to reprint 'The Sunrise' from *Bluebeard's Egg* by Margaret Atwood, 1987.

The Estate of Angela Carter, care of Rogers, Coleridge & White Ltd, 20 Powis Mews, London W11 1JN for permission to reprint 'The Quilt Maker' from *Burning Your Boats* by Angela Carter. Copyright © The Estate of Angela Carter 1995.

Little, Brown for permission to reprint 'The Bishop's Lunch' from *During Mother's Absence* by Michèle Roberts, 1994.

Kali for Women for permission to reprint 'Hand-me-downs' by Wajida Tabassum, translated by Manisha Chaudhry, from *Truth Tales 2: The Slate of Life*, 1991.

Sara Maitland for permission to reprint 'The Loveliness of the Long-Distance Runner', 1979.

Carol Mara for permission to reprint 'Lipstick, Stockings, Bras and Sex' from *Eva's Crossing*, 1993.

Onlywomen Press for permission to reprint 'Below Zero' by Alison Ward from *In and Out of Time* edited by Patricia Dunker, 1990.

Penguin Books (NZ) for permission to reprint 'Harp Music' from *The Sky People* by Patricia Grace, 1995.

Random House Inc for permission to reprint 'Sweet Town' from

Permissions

Gorilla, My Love by Toni Cade Bambara. Copyright © Toni Cade Bambara 1959.

The Estate of Alma Routsong, care of Abner Stein, for permission to reprint 'The Outsider' from *A Dooryard Full of Flowers* by Isabel Miller, 1994.

Scribner, a Division of Simon & Schuster, for permission to reprint 'Two Words' from *The Stories of Eva Luna* by Isabel Allende, translated by Margaret Sayers Peden. Copyright © Isabel Allende 1989. English translation copyright © Macmillan Publishing Company.

Seal Press for permission to reprint 'In the Deep Heart's Core' from *Lovers' Choice* by Becky Birtha, 1988.

Kathleen Tyau, care of Peters, Fraser & Dunlop, for permission to reprint 'Pick Up Your Pine' from *A Little Too Much Is Enough*, 1996.

Alice Walker, care of David Higham Associates, for permission to reprint 'A Sudden Trip Home in the Spring' from *You Can't Keep a Good Woman Down*, 1984.

CONTENTS

INTRODUCTION

Sunrise to Sunset gathers together a compelling collection of
women's short stories evoking summer. When making my selec-
tion I looked for stories that reflect the diversity of women's lives;
that refresh, stimulate and entertain; and that make the quiet
moments of summer all the richer.

The long hot days of childhood and adolescence are potent
images of summer reflected in several of the stories here: Kathleen
Tyau's fast-paced tale tells us of Mahealani's first summer job in
a hectic pineapple factory; Carol Mara's Moira finds out what sex
is all about from her friend Margaret's drawings on the school
toilet walls; Isabel Miller's Rebecca tells us about emotional
honesty in adults; and Toni Cade Bambara's Kit discovers 'a
certain glandular disturbance' all her own.

Elsewhere in *Sunrise to Sunset*, it is in maturity that the problems of youth can be resolved: in 'Harp Music' an elderly woman,
attending her grandchildren's school fête, finds the quiet beauty
of the child she once was – a discovery that helps her face the
future with a new independence. Becky Birtha's Sahara, on
the road again for the first time since her teens, encounters a
young runaway, and in acting to protect her comes to terms
with her own troubled adolescence. In 'Hand-me-downs' Chamki,
entering womanhood, enacts a revenge denied her in childhood.
And Michèle Roberts' Sister Josephine prepares a miraculous
feast for the Bishop's Easter visit, and is led to reevaluate her
mother's advice and dramatically rethink her career.

In other stories, dramatic landscapes provide a backdrop to

stories of love and loss: Isabel Allende's Belisa Crepusculario
seduces the rebel Colonel with two words in the South American
mountains; in Bonnie Burnard's story, a woman takes leave of
the man she loves and of the young boy who has grown too
close, on a walk up a 'grizzly' mountain; and in 'Below Zero' a
filmmaker tells of her bittersweet trip to the Arctic to record Dr
Thea Christiansen and the dinosaur bones she has excavated.

Meanwhile, back in the city, we learn the secret of Margaret
Atwood's Yvonne (for surely, she must have one if she is single,
independent and happy!). Alice Walker's student, Sarah, discovers that gaining an education in a white, northern college
does not have to separate her from her black, southern family.
In Angela Carter's 'The Quilt Maker' a forty-year-old woman
reevaluates the 'crazy patchwork' of her life as the eighty-year-
old woman next door goes into hospital, apparently unable to
look after herself. And Sara Maitland's Sally learns the nature of
compromise and understanding through love, as her partner Jane
completes the London marathon.

Together these stories are like a long summer day, a sharply lit
look at women's lives.

Charlotte Cole

Two Words

ISABEL ALLENDE

SHE WENT by the name of Belisa Crepusculario, not because she had been baptized with that name or given it by her mother, but because she herself had searched until she found the poetry of 'beauty' and 'twilight' and cloaked herself in it. She made her living selling words. She journeyed through the country from the high cold mountains to the burning coasts, stopping at fairs and in markets where she set up four poles covered by a canvas awning under which she took refuge from the sun and rain to minister to her customers. She did not have to peddle her merchandise because from having wandered far and near, everyone knew who she was. Some people waited for her from one year to the next, and when she appeared in the village with her bundle beneath her arm, they would form a line in front of her stall. Her prices were fair. For five centavos she delivered verses from memory; for seven she improved the quality of dreams; for nine she wrote love letters; for twelve she invented insults for irreconcilable enemies. She also sold stories, not fantasies but long, true stories she recited at one telling, never skipping a word. This is how she carried the news from one town to another. People paid her to add a line or two: our son was born; so and so died; our children got married; the crops burned in the field. Wherever she went a small crowd gathered around to listen as she began to speak, and that was how they learned about each others' doings, about distant relatives, about what was going on in the civil war. To anyone who paid her fifty centavos in trade, she gave the gift of a secret word to drive away melancholy. It was not the same word for everyone, naturally, because that would have been collective deceit. Each person received his or her own word, with the assurance that no one else would use it that way in this universe or the beyond.

Belisa Crepusculario had been born into a family so poor they did not even have names to give their children. She came into the world and grew up in an inhospitable land where some years the rains became avalanches of water that bore everything away before them and others when not a drop fell from the sky and the sun swelled to fill the horizon and the world became a desert. Until she was twelve, Belisa had no occupation or virtue other than having withstood hunger and the exhaustion of centuries. During one interminable drought, it fell to her to bury four younger brothers and sisters; when she realized that her turn was next, she decided to set out across the plains in the direction of the sea, in hopes that she might trick death along the way. The land was eroded, split with deep cracks, strewn with rocks, fossils of trees and thorny bushes, and skeletons of animals bleached by the sun. From time to time she ran into families who, like her, were heading south, following the mirage of water. Some had begun the march carrying their belongings on their back or in small carts, but they could barely move their own bones, and after a while they had to abandon their possessions. They dragged themselves along painfully, their skin turned to lizard hide and their eyes burned by the reverberating glare. Belisa greeted them with a wave as she passed, but she did not stop, because she had no strength to waste in acts of compassion. Many people fell by the wayside, but she was so stubborn that she survived to cross through that hell and at long last reach the first trickles of water, fine, almost invisible threads that fed spindly vegetation and farther down widened into small streams and marshes.

Belisa Crepusculario saved her life and in the process accidentally discovered writing. In a village near the coast, the wind blew a page of newspaper at her feet. She picked up the brittle yellow paper and stood a long while looking at it, unable to determine its purpose, until curiosity overcame her shyness. She walked over to a man who was washing his horse in the muddy pool where she had quenched her thirst.

'What is this?' she asked.

'The sports page of the newspaper,' the man replied, concealing his surprise at her ignorance.

The answer astounded the girl, but she did not want to seem rude so she merely inquired about the significance of the fly tracks scattered across the page.

'Those are words, child. Here it says that Fulgencio Barba knocked out El Negro Tiznao in the third round.'

That was the day Belisa Crepusculario found out that words make their way in the world without a master, and that anyone with a little cleverness can appropriate them and do business with them. She made a quick assessment of her situation and concluded that aside from becoming a prostitute or working as a servant in the kitchens of the rich there were few occupations she was qualified for. It seemed to her that selling words would be an honourable alternative. From that moment on, she worked at that profession, and was never tempted by any other. At the beginning, she offered her merchandise unaware that words could be written outside of newspapers. When she learned otherwise, she calculated the infinite possibilities of her trade and with her savings paid a priest twenty pesos to teach her to read and write; with her three remaining coins she bought a dictionary. She pored over it from A to Z and then threw it into the sea, because it was not her intention to defraud her customers with packaged words.

One August morning several years later, Belisa Crepusculario was sitting in her tent in the middle of a plaza, surrounded by the uproar of market day, selling legal arguments to an old man who had been trying for sixteen years to get his pension. Suddenly she heard yelling and thudding hoofbeats. She looked up from her writing and saw, first, a cloud of dust, and then a band of horsemen come galloping into the plaza. They were the Colonel's men, sent under orders of El Mulato, a giant known throughout the land for the speed of his knife and his loyalty to his chief. Both the Colonel and El Mulato had spent their lives fighting in the civil war, and their names were ineradicably linked to devastation and calamity. The rebels swept into town like a stampeding herd, wrapped in noise, bathed in sweat, and leaving a hurricane of fear in their trail. Chickens took wing, dogs ran for their lives, women and children scurried out of sight, until the only living soul left in the market was Belisa Crepusculario. She had never seen El Mulato and was surprised to see him walking towards her.

'I'm looking for you,' he shouted, pointing his coiled whip at her; even before the words were out, two men rushed her – knocking over her canopy and shattering her inkwell – bound her hand and foot, and threw her like a duffel bag across the rump of El Mulato's mount. Then they thundered off towards the hills.

Hours later, just as Belisa Crepusculario was near death, her heart ground to sand by the pounding of the horse, they stopped, and four strong hands set her down. She tried to stand on her feet and hold her head high, but her strength failed her and she slumped to the ground, sinking into a confused dream. She awakened several hours later to the murmur of night in the camp, but before she had time to sort out the sounds, she opened her eyes and found herself staring into the impatient glare of El Mulato, kneeling beside her.

'Well, woman, at last you have come to,' he said. To speed her to her senses, he tipped his canteen and offered her a sip of liquor laced with gunpowder.

She demanded to know the reason for such rough treatment, and El Mulato explained that the Colonel needed her services. He allowed her to splash water on her face, and then led her to the far end of the camp where the most feared man in all the land was lazing in a hammock strung between two trees. She could not see his face, because he lay in the deceptive shadow of the leaves and the indelible shadow of all his years as a bandit, but she imagined from the way his gigantic aide addressed him with such humility that he must have a very menacing expression. She was surprised by the Colonel's voice, as soft and well modulated as a professor's.

'Are you the woman who sells words?' he asked.

'At your service,' she stammered, peering into the dark and trying to see him better.

The Colonel stood up, and turned straight towards her. She saw dark skin and the eyes of a ferocious puma, and she knew immediately that she was standing before the loneliest man in the world.

'I want to be President,' he announced.

The Colonel was weary of riding across that godforsaken land, waging useless wars and suffering defeats that no subterfuge could transform into victories. For years he had been sleeping in the open air, bitten by mosquitoes, eating iguanas and snake soup, but those minor inconveniences were not why he wanted to change his destiny. What truly troubled him was the terror he saw in people's eyes. He longed to ride into a town beneath a triumphal arch with bright flags and flowers everywhere; he wanted to be cheered, and be given newly laid eggs and freshly baked bread. Men fled at the sight of him, children trembled, and women miscarried from fright; he had had enough, and so he had decided to become President. El Mulato had suggested that they ride to the capital, gallop up to the Palace, and take over the government, the way they had taken so many other things without anyone's permission. The Colonel, however, did not want to be just another tyrant; there had been enough of those before him and, besides, if he did that, he would never win people's hearts. It was his aspiration to win the popular vote in the December elections.

'To do that, I have to talk like a candidate. Can you sell me the words for a speech?' the Colonel asked Belisa Crepusculario.

She had accepted many assignments, but none like this. She did not dare refuse, fearing that El Mulato would shoot her between the eyes, or worse still, that the Colonel would burst into tears. There was more to it than that, however; she felt the urge to help him because she felt a throbbing warmth beneath her skin, a powerful desire to touch that man, to fondle him, to clasp him in her arms.

All night and a good part of the following day, Belisa Crepusculario searched her repertory for words adequate for a presidential speech, closely watched by El Mulato, who could not take his eyes from her firm wanderer's legs and virginal breasts. She discarded harsh, cold words, words that were too flowery, words worn from abuse, words that offered improbable promises, untruthful and confusing words, until all she had left were words sure to touch the minds of men and women's intuition. Calling upon the knowledge she had purchased from the priest for twenty pesos, she wrote the speech on a sheet of paper and then signalled El Mulato to untie the rope that bound her ankles to a tree. He led her once more to the Colonel, and again she felt the throbbing anxiety that had seized her when she first saw him. She handed him the paper and waited while he looked at it, holding it gingerly between thumbs and fingertips.

'What the shit does this say?' he asked finally.

'Don't you know how to read?'

'War's what I know,' he replied.

She read the speech aloud. She read it three times, so her client could engrave it on his memory. When she finished, she saw the emotion in the faces of the soldiers who had gathered round to listen, and saw that the Colonel's eyes glittered with enthusiasm, convinced that with those words the presidential chair would be his.

'If after they've heard it three times, the boys are still standing there with their mouths hanging open, it must mean the thing's damn good, Colonel,' was El Mulato's approval.

'All right, woman. How much do I owe you?' the leader asked.

'One peso, Colonel.'

'That's not much,' he said, opening the purse he wore at his belt, heavy with proceeds from the last foray.

'The peso entitles you to a bonus. I'm going to give you two secret words,' said Belisa Crepusculario.

'What for?'

She explained that for every fifty centavos a client paid, she gave him the gift of a word for his exclusive use. The Colonel shrugged. He had no interest at all in her offer, but he did not want to be impolite to someone who had served him so well. She walked slowly to the leather stool where he was sitting, and bent down to give him her gift. The man smelled the scent of a mountain cat issuing from the woman, a fiery heat radiating from her hips, he heard the terrible whisper of her hair, and a breath of sweet mint murmured into his ear the two secret words that were his alone.

'They are yours, Colonel,' she said as she stepped back. 'You may use them as much as you please.'

El Mulato accompanied Belisa to the roadside, his eyes as entreating as a stray dog's, but when he reached out to touch her, he was stopped by an avalanche of words he had never heard before; believing them to be an irrevocable curse, the flame of his desire was extinguished.

During the months of September, October and November, the Colonel delivered his speech so many times that had it not been crafted from glowing and durable words, it would have turned to ash as he spoke. He travelled up and down and across the country, riding into cities with a triumphal air, stopping in even the most forgotten villages where only the dump heap betrayed a human presence, to convince his fellow citizens to vote for him. While he spoke from a platform erected in the middle of the plaza, El Mulato and his men handed out sweets and painted his name on all the walls in gold frost. No one paid the least attention to those advertising ploys; they were dazzled by the clarity of the Colonel's proposals and the poetic lucidity of his arguments, infected by his powerful wish to right the wrongs of history, happy for the first time in their lives. When the Candidate had finished his speech, his soldiers would fire their pistols into the air and set off firecrackers, and when finally they rode off, they left behind a wake of hope that lingered for days on the air, like the

splendid memory of a comet's tail. Soon the Colonel was
the favourite. No one had ever witnessed such a phenomenon: a
man who surfaced from the civil war, covered with scars and
speaking like a professor, a man whose fame spread to every
corner of the land and captured the nation's heart. The press
focused their attention on him. Newspapermen came from far
away to interview him and repeat his phrases, and the number
of his followers and enemies continued to grow.

'We're doing great, Colonel,' said El Mulato, after twelve successful weeks of campaigning.

But the Candidate did not hear. He was repeating his secret
words, as he did more and more obsessively. He said them when
he was mellow with nostalgia; he murmured them in his sleep; he
carried them with him on horseback; he thought them before
delivering his famous speech; and he caught himself savouring
them in his leisure time. And every time he thought of those
two words, he thought of Belisa Crepusculario, and his senses
were inflamed with the memory of her feral scent, her fiery heat,
the whisper of her hair and her sweet mint breath in his ear,
until he began to go around like a sleepwalker, and his men
realized that he might die before he ever sat in the presidential
chair.

'What's got hold of you, Colonel?' El Mulato asked so often
that finally one day his chief broke down and told him the source
of his befuddlement: those two words that were buried like two
daggers in his gut.

'Tell me what they are and maybe they'll lose their magic,' his
faithful aide suggested.

'I can't tell them, they're for me alone,' the Colonel replied.

Saddened by watching his chief decline like a man with a
death sentence on his head, El Mulato slung his rifle over his
shoulder and set out to find Belisa Crepusculario. He followed
her trail through all that vast country, until he found her in a
village in the far south, sitting under her tent reciting her rosary
of news. He planted himself, straddle-legged, before her, weapon
in hand.

'You! You're coming with me,' he ordered.

She had been waiting. She picked up her inkwell, folded the canvas of her small stall, arranged her shawl around her shoulders, and without a word took her place behind El Mulato's saddle. They did not exchange so much as a word in all the trip; El Mulato's desire for her had turned into rage, and only his fear of her tongue prevented his cutting her to shreds with his whip. Nor was he inclined to tell her that the Colonel was in a fog, and that a spell whispered into his ear had done what years of battle had not been able to do. Three days later they arrived at the encampment, and immediately, in view of all the troops, El Mulato led his prisoner before the Candidate.

'I brought this witch here so you can give her back her words, Colonel,' El Mulato said, pointing the barrel of his rifle at the woman's head. 'And then she can give you back your manhood.'

The Colonel and Belisa Crepusculario stared at each other, measuring one another from a distance. The men knew then that their leader would never undo the witchcraft of those two accursed words, because the whole world could see the voracious puma's eyes soften as the woman walked to him and took his hand in hers.

From *The Stories of Eva Luna*, published by Penguin.

Sweet Town

TONI CADE BAMBARA

IT IS hard to believe that there was only one spring and one summer apiece that year, my fifteenth year. It is hard to believe that I so quickly squandered my youth in the sweet town playground of the sunny city, that wild monkeybardom of my fourth-grade youthhood. However, it was so.

'Dear Mother' – I wrote one day on her bathroom mirror with a candle sliver – 'please forgive my absence and my decay and overlook the freckled dignity and pockmarked integrity plaguing me this season.'

I used to come on even wilder sometimes and write her mad cryptic notes on the kitchen sink with charred matches. Anything for a bit, we so seldom saw each other. I even sometimes wrote her a note on paper. And then one day, having romped my soul through the spectrum of sunny colors, I dashed up to her apartment to escape the heat and found a letter from her which eternally elated my heart to the point of bursture and generally endeared her to me forever. Written on the kitchen table in cake frosting was the message, 'My dear, mad, perverse young girl, kindly take care and paint the fire escape in your leisure . . .' All the i's were dotted with marmalade, the t's were crossed with orange rind. Here was a sight to carry with one forever in the back of the screaming eyeballs somewhere. I howled for at least five minutes out of sheer madity and vowed to love her completely. Leisure. As if bare-armed spring ever let up from its invitation to perpetuate the race. And as if we ever owned a fire escape. 'Zweep,' I yelled, not giving a damn for intelligibility and decided that if ever I was to run away from home, I'd take her with me. And with that in mind, and with Penelope splintering through the landscape and the pores secreting animal champagne, I bent my youth to the season's tempo and proceeded to lose my mind.

There is a certain glandular disturbance all beautiful, wizardy, great people have second sight to, that trumpets through the clothes, sets the nerves up for the kill, and torments the senses to orange explosure. It has something to do with the cosmic interrelationship between the cellular atunement of certain designated organs and the firmental correlation with the axis shifts of the globe. My mother calls it sex and my brother says it's groin-fever time. But then, they were always ones for brevity. Anyway, that's the way it was. And in this spring race, the glands always win and the muses and the brain core must step aside to ride in the trunk with the spare tire. It was during this sweet and drugged madness time that I met BJ, wearing his handsomeness like an article of clothing, for an effect, and wearing his friend Eddie like a necessary pimple of adolescence. It was on the beach that we met, me looking great in a pair of cut-off dungarees and them with beards. Never mind the snows of yesteryear, I told myself, I'll take the sand and sun blizzard any day.

'Listen, Kit,' said BJ to me one night after we had experienced such we-encounters with the phenomenal world at large as a two-strawed mocha, duo-jaywalking summons, twosome whistling scenes, and other such like we-experiences, 'the thing for us to do is hitch to the Coast and get into films.'

'Righto,' said Ed. 'And soon.'

'Sure thing, honeychile,' I said, and jumped over an unknown garbage can. 'We were made for celluloid – beautifully chiseld are we, not to mention well-buffed.' I ran up and down somebody's stoop, whistling 'Columbia the Gem of the Ocean' through my nose. And Eddie made siren sounds and walked a fence. BJ grasped a parking-sign pole and extended himself parallel to the ground. I applauded, not only the gymnastics but also the offer. We liked to make bold directionless overtures to action like those crazy teenagers you're always running into on the printed page or MGM movies.

'We could buy a sleeping bag,' said BJ, and challenged a store cat to duel.

'We could buy a sleeping bag,' echoed Eddie, who never had any real contribution to make in the say of statements.

'Three in a bag,' I said while BJ grasped me by the belt and we went flying down a side street. 'Hrumph,' I coughed, and perched on a fire hydrant. 'Only one bag?'

'Of course,' said BJ.

'Of course,' said Ed. 'And hrumph.'

We came on like this the whole summer, even crazier. All of our friends abandoned us, they couldn't keep the pace. My mother threatened me with disinheritance. And my old roommate from camp actually turned the hose on me one afternoon in a fit of Florence Nightingale therapy. But hand in hand, me and Pan, and Eddie too, whizzed through the cement kaleidoscope making our own crazy patterns, singing our own song. And then one night a crazy thing happened. I dreamt that BJ was running down the street howling, tearing his hair out and making love to the garbage cans on the boulevard. I was there laughing my head off and Eddie was spinning a beer bottle with a faceless person I didn't even know. I woke up and screamed for no reason I know of and my roommate, who was living with us, threw a Saltine cracker at me in way of saying something about silence, peace, consideration, and sleepdom. And then on top of that another crazy thing happened. Pebbles were flying into my opened window. The whole thing struck me funny. It wasn't a casement window and there was no garden underneath. I naturally laughed my head off and my roommate got really angry and cursed me out viciously. I explained to her that pebbles were coming in, but she wasn't one for imagination and turned over into sleepdom. I went to the window to see who I was going to share my balcony scene with, and there below, standing on the milkbox, was BJ. I climbed out and joined him on the stoop.

'What's up?' I asked, ready to take the world by storm in my mixed-match baby-doll pajamas. BJ motioned me into the foyer and I could see by the distraught mask that he was wearing that serious discussion was afoot.

'Listen, Kit,' he began, looking both ways with unnecessary caution. 'We're leaving, tonight, now. Me and Eddie. He stole some money from his grandmother, so we're cutting out.'

'Where're ya going?' I asked. He shrugged. And just then I saw Eddie dash across the stoop and into the shadows. BJ shrugged and he made some kind of desperate sound with his voice like a stifled cry. 'It's been real great. The summer and you . . . but . . .'

'Look here,' I said with anger. 'I don't know why the hell you want to hang around with that nothing.' I was really angry but sorry too. It wasn't at all what I wanted to say. I would have liked to have said, 'Apollo, we are the only beautiful people in the world. And because our genes are so great, our kid can't help but burst through the human skin into cosmic significance.' I wanted to say, 'You will bear in mind that I am great, brilliant, talented, good-looking, and am going to college at fifteen. I have the most interesting complexes ever, and despite Freud and Darwin I have made a healthy adjustment as an earthworm.' But I didn't tell him this. Instead, I revealed that petty, small, mean side of me by saying 'Eddie is a shithead.'

BJ scratched his head, swung his foot in an arc, groaned and took off. 'Maybe next summer . . .' he started to say but his voice cracked and he and Eddie went dashing down the night street, arm in arm. I stood there with my thighs bare and my soul shook. Maybe we will meet next summer, I told the mailboxes. Or maybe I'll quit school and bum around the country. And in every town I'll ask for them as the hotel keeper feeds the dusty, weary traveler that I'll be. 'Have you seen two guys, one great, the other acned? If you see 'em, tell 'em Kit's looking for them.' And I'd bandage up my cactus-torn feet and sling the knapsack into place and be off. And in the next town, having endured dust storms, tornadoes, earthquakes, and coyotes, I'll stop at the saloon and inquire. 'Yeh, they travel together,' I'd say in a voice somewhere between WC Fields and Gladys Cooper. 'Great buddies. Inseparable. Tell 'em for me that Kit's still a great kid.'

And legends'll pop up about me and my quest. Great long twelve-bar blues ballads with eighty-nine stanzas. And a strolling minstrel will happen into the feedstore where BJ'll be and hear and shove the farmer's daughter off his lap and mount up to find me. Or maybe we won't meet ever, or we will but I won't recognize him cause he'll be an enchanted frog or a bald-headed fat man and I'll be God knows what. No matter. Days other than the here and now, I told myself, will be dry and sane and sticky with the rotten apricots oozing slowly in the sweet time of my betrayed youth.

From *Gorilla, My Love*, published by The Women's Press.

Pick Up Your Pine

KATHLEEN TYAU

AUNTY HANNAH Mele got me the job in the pineapple cannery this summer. She got me the job because she has pull. Connections, pull, at least twenty years of pull – first as a packer, then as a trimmer, and now as forelady on one of the lines. Just tell the boss you're my niece, she said. Tell him you're fast. Tell him you're good.

Pineapple ripening red and gold in the fields, pineapple waiting to be picked. Waiting for the pickers to snap off their crowns. Crowns off and pineapples rolling onto the belts, into the trucks. Rolling, poking and shoving with thorny skins, out of my way, out of my way. Pineapple ripe and rolling onto the belts, into the trucks, poking and shoving their way to the cannery in town, near the wharf.

I wait for the 5:30 bus in front of the mama-san, papa-san store down by the highway that goes into town. My jeans rustle as I pace in front of the store in the cool morning air. My jeans are stiff and very blue, and I have to roll up the cuffs four times. Even though it's still dark, papa-san has already opened the store. I long to buy something from the crackseed rack – a bag of cherry seed or red coconut balls. Something sweet to add to my lunch. My mother has packed me a bologna sandwich on brown Love's bread and a Red Delicious apple. But I haven't earned any money yet, and the bus pulls up, the inside lights still on. I sit in the front, close to the driver. I press my face against the glass, watch for my stop, the building with the giant pineapple sitting on top.

15

Pineapple coming in from the fields, poking and shoving, and smelling ripe. The smell of ripe pineapple filling the air, falling thick and warm as a blanket. When the bus stops at the cannery, I can smell where I am.

Aunty Hannah Mele waves at me as I walk past her line. See you lunchtime, she says. She is one of my Hawaiian aunties, married to my goong goong's youngest brother. A tall, regal woman with long hair piled on her head like a crown. If not for the hairnet holding down her hair, I know it would glow. Girls, she says to the women sitting on stools, this is my niece Mahealani. Mahi, say hello. But these are not girls. Many of them are as old as she is, older than my mother, way older than me.

The whistle blows. Six-thirty. The boy feeds pine one by one to the genaka machine. The girls check him out. They shout, Oh da cute, but he cannot hear them. Oh da cute kine guy, our genaka boy is cuter than the others. Pineapple falling out of the genaka, pineapple rolling down the line, where the girls are shouting, where the girls are singing. Our pine is sweeter, our line is faster, the best in the whole cannery, no ka oi, no ka oi. Pineapple marching one by one down the line where the trimmers and packers wait. Pineapple with their cores removed and their skins chopped off. Pineapple already looking like cans.

I am a trimmer, and I will earn a nickel more than the packers. I'm not on Aunty Hannah Mele's line. I'm on my own and have my own forelady. She sees my red badge. Red instead of white, so she knows, so everybody knows, I am a child laborer, not yet sixteen.

Pineapples marching in front of me now. I sit at the front of the line, where the pine falls out of the genaka machine. Pick up your pine, pick up your pine, the forelady shouts, as the trimmers trim and the packers pack. The trimmers trim the eyes still staring from the pine, eyes that the genaka has missed, eyes that must not go in the cans. Roll the pineapple around on your thumb. Then make diagonal slashes across the pine with your knife. See the eyes fall out, four, five at a time. See how fast, that's what you want. No time to cut out one eye at a time. Then put the pineapple back on the line. Pick up your pine, pick up your pine.

You have to catch every one of the pine. Cut off the eyes before they get away. Cannot let even one slip by. So roll the pine faster on your thumb until your thumb muscle aches, and you see it swell and you see it grow and you wonder if your muscle will burst. Only half an hour has gone by and your thumb is already sore. One week sore, one month sore, sore and swelling, sore and aching, when will it stop? When will it stop?

The women next to me are singing, but I don't know the words. I can hear only the chopping of the genakas and the grinding of the belts and the clanking of the cans. And the forelady shouts from behind, Pick up your pine, pick up your pine. Other hands reach for the pine, but not mine. I am trying to spin a whole pineapple on my thumb. The forelady yells, paces up and down, finally yanks me from my stool at the front of the line and moves me to the end of the row of trimmers. She points at a plastic tub. She makes the words big in her mouth: Fill. It. Up. I remove pineapples from the belt that the trimmers have missed because they are one girl short, because of me. I grab the pineapples before they reach the slicing machine. Haul them to the front of the line where the faster trimmers trim. Eyes left and right flying off the pine. The girls are singing, knife blades flashing, and I am catching pine.

Pineapple twirling on thumbs, knives slashing, eyes falling into the trough, cans and belts clattering, banging. And the marching pineapples marching down the line, from the trimmers to the slicing machine, from the slicer to the packers, from the packers to the cans. And all the way down the line, the forelady cries, Pick up your pine, pick up your pine.

The forelady pulls me from the line again. The whole line moves up a seat, including one of the packers. I move to the front of the line of packers. Next to the machine where the slices fall out. What about my extra nickel an hour? Are they going to pay me as a packer or a trimmer? A dollar quarter doesn't feel as good as a dollar thirty, but now I have to pick up only three or four slices of pine at a time. Neat, beautiful Life Saver slices, falling like fresh bread out of the bag. Looking even less like pineapples and more like cans now. Twelve or more slices at a time. Slices to admire, to toss into cans waiting on trays. Trays that the tray boys haul away.

But first you must decide. See the dark yellow slices, the translucent yellow, those are number one. All the rest are number two or three. If really bad, then number three, but try not to have number three. See the white flecks, the solid yellow. No flecks in number one, so this is two. Two not as sweet, but still good. Three is the worst, so you don't want three. Not as good money as one and two. Good lines have more number one. Number one is the best, no ka oi, no ka oi.

I stand at the best place in the line of packers. At the front, first in line, where I can scoop up all the number ones. I can pick up ones all day, smile, think how beautiful, how sweet the cans I've packed. Next time we go to the store I'll know how to look for the number-one cans. But the forelady yells at me, Pick up the rest! Pick them all up! The first four slices are easy, but not the ones that follow.

Pick up your pine, pick up your pine, the forelady shouts, and the trimmers trim and the packers pack and their lips mouth the words of the music trying to drown out the genaka machines. Knife blades flash to the beat, cans bang in the trays, and the pineapples march down the line, down the line.

Why have I never noticed ones and twos before? What if I put a two in a one can or a three in a two can? If a one goes in with a two, will they know? If a three becomes a two and a two becomes a one, then which is really a two, which is really a one? How do you know? How do you know?

The packer next to me on the line picks up all the slices I miss. She packs faster than I can think, and her cans fill up with number ones. Twos and threes evaporate. She sees what I cannot see fast enough. The forelady yanks me from where I am frozen, sticks me at the end of the line again, gives me a plastic tub.

Points. I know. I pick up the slices the packers can't pack in time. Catch them before they fall into the trough and go where the trimmings go, to the juice, to the juice. To the juice, and what a waste of good pine.

Stop the line? Never happen. Never heard of such thing. Not this line, not my line. The forelady grabs the tub from me, and she and the first packer empty out the bin. Slices fly out of their hands and into the cans. Number one, number two. Number two, number three. Number one, so easy; number two, just like breathing.

Pick up your pine, pick up your pine, and don't get juice on your arms, don't get juice in your eyes. The juice can make your skin break. The juice can make your skin bleed, and you will have to go to the infirmary, and the nurse will wrap your arms in gauze, long strips of gauze, and everyone will know you were careless. Get juice in your eyes and she'll call an ambulance. The juice can make you blind. This is no joke, this is no joke.

A splash on my arm. A small squirt of juice. No, no, not me, but I show the forelady. Hold out my arm like it's diseased, not mine. She points to the infirmary, and the pine keeps rolling and the slices keep flying, and the nurse washes off my arm with lots and lots of soap and water. I don't see blood, I am lucky this time, but you can't take a chance. I stare at my arm, at the inch of raw skin turning pink, turning red. Is it the blood churning below? Is it the blood waiting to flow? Just one square inch of pink on my arm, and the nurse wraps my whole forearm in six inches of gauze. Six! All the way up to my elbow. Did you get any juice on the other one too? I shake my head no. But she checks, sees a little pink, wraps that one up too, just in case, just in case. But no juice in my eyes, so back to the line.

Back to the line, but I can't pack now. Can't pack, can't trim, too slow, can't get close to the pine with gauze on both arms, so the forelady makes me sweep. Get the broom, sweep the floor, let them see who you are. Let them see the gauze, see the badge. A red badge because still fifteen, a red badge and white gauze, gauze that hides blood. No more trimming and packing today for you. One arm wrapped in gauze is bad enough, but two. Two means you have to sweep the floor and everybody knows who you are.

The whistle blows. Eleven. Half an hour for lunch and only a half day gone. I spend ten minutes walking quickly to the locker room, taking off my gloves, washing my hands, using the toilet. I will need ten minutes to powder my hands and put the gloves back on. That leaves me ten minutes to eat. So walk fast to the cafeteria, where Aunty Hannah Mele sits. Waiting for me. She holds out a frosty can of guava juice. Oh, you got hurt, poor thing, but no worry, you will be okay, come and sit by me. You want a bite of my tuna fish? She gives me a piece of kulolo she has steamed the night before. She knows it's my favorite. She gives me some to eat now, some wrapped in foil to put in my locker and take home. I bite off chunks of the chewy taro pudding, savor the sweet taste of coconut milk.

After lunch the forelady sends me up the ladder. I climb way up, way above the packers and the trimmers, above the conveyor belts and genakas. I climb up the ladder and crawl across the catwalk over to the big chute. Everything that falls into the troughs passes through this chute. The pineapple pulp and the pineapple skin, the pineapple cores and the pineapple eyes, all the trimmings, all of it falling, falling out of the chute. Falling so fast I cannot see what is what. My job is to catch the knives, the knives that fall in the trough. The knives in this mess? The knives falling fast? But how can I see them? How can I catch them? Look for the blades, look for the shiny part of the knives. Catch them before they fall into the juice, before they jam up the machine and the whole cannery has to shut down, shut down. Grab them by the handle, not the blade, or you'll get cut and your fingers, your hands might fall into the juice, into the juice. Sit and watch everything falling, everything flying, and try not to think about what you heard at lunch about the boy whose arm got caught in the genaka machine. Where did the arm go? Into the trough? Into the chute? Did it get in the juice? Don't miss, don't catch the knife wrong or they will have to stop the lines and close the place down because of you, because of you. And who knows what will happen to the juice, all of it turning red. Red, po ho, what a waste.

I catch two knives. Two, by the handle. Two very smart very fast good eyes saved the juice. Saved the juice. Everything is falling, flying by, and I see it all and I do not see anything. I do not see what I am seeing, and my eyes are so tired, and I am so dizzy, and how did I catch them? How did the knives get up here? How did *I* get up here? I'm afraid I will fall into the pulp, fall into the juice. Where is the forelady, why doesn't she come? Everybody down there, working the line, will they forget about me up here? My head banging, my body shaking, and the whole cannery rushes by, rushes by.

The whistle blows. Three o'clock. Pau work. Silence except for rubber gloves snapping, feet shuffling, the girls saying goodbye. A kiss from Aunty Hannah Mele as I walk past her line. A kiss on my stink face. Don't worry about the arms. You'll be better tomorrow. So stink and the bus is already crowded and who wants to stand next to me. Not me. Stink and tired and hot and I want to sit down, lie down and go to sleep and never get up. Don't want to touch anybody. Don't want them to smell me, so hauna, so hauna. People get on the bus at every stop. They sit down, then stand up for anyone older than them. When one gets up and one sits down, all the people standing on the bus have to move. Move to the back, move to the back, the bus driver yells. Some people get off, some move to the front, some move to the back. Sit down, stand up, all the way home. I know they can smell the pineapple on me, on my clothes. Overripe pineapple, rotting in the sun. My jeans are no longer stiff, my cuffs unroll, shirt sticks to my back. The gauze itches my skin, and I want to scratch, scratch, scratch it all off.

Long walk up the hill in the afternoon sun. Take a bath, eat, fall into bed at eight. Pineapples still marching across the lawn, pineapples walking on the stone wall, fingers, legs falling into perfect slices on my plate. The forelady shouting, Pick up your pine, pick up your pine. I give up my seat on the bus to number one.

No pineapple in my fruit cocktail. This pineapple isn't ripe. Can't you see the yellow is wrong? No pineapple juice for me. Rub it with salt before you eat. No pineapple on my pizza. Wash your mouth, wash your hands before they bleed. No pineapple in my mai tai. No piña colada, please.

From A *Little Too Much Is Enough*, published by The Women's Press.

The Sunrise

MARGARET ATWOOD

YVONNE FOLLOWS men. She does this discreetly and at a distance, at first; usually she spots them on the subway, where she has the leisure to sit down and look about her, but sometimes she will pass one on the street and turn and walk along behind him, hurrying a little to keep up. Occasionally she rides the subway or goes walking just for this purpose, but more often the sighting is accidental. Once she's made it, though, she postpones whatever she's doing and makes a detour. This has caused her to miss appointments, which bothers her because she's punctual as a rule.

On the subway, Yvonne takes care not to stare too hard: she doesn't want to frighten anyone. When the man gets off the train, Yvonne gets off too and walks to the exit with him, several yards behind. At this point she will either follow him home to see where he lives and lie in wait for him some other day, when she's made up her mind about him, or she'll speak to him once they're out on the street. Two or three times a man has realized he's being shadowed. One actually began to run. Another turned to confront her, back against a nearby drugstore window, as if cornered. One headed for a crowd and lost her in it. These, she thinks, are the ones with guilty consciences.

When the time is right, Yvonne quickens her pace, comes up beside the man, and touches him on the arm. She always says the same thing:

'Excuse me. You're going to find this strange, but I'd like to draw you. Please don't mistake this for a sexual advance.'

Then there's an interval, during which they say *What?* and Yvonne explains. There's no charge, she says, and no strings. She just wants to draw them. They don't have to take their clothes off if they don't want to; the head and shoulders will do nicely. She really is a professional artist. She is not mad.

If they've listened to her initial appeal at all, and most do, it's very hard for them to say no. What does she want from them, after all? Only a small amount of their time, so that they can let her have access to something only they can give. They've been singled out as unique, told they are not interchangeable. No one knows better than Yvonne how seductive this is. Most of them say yes.

Yvonne isn't interested in men who are handsome in the ordinary way: she's not drawing toothpaste ads. Besides, men with capped-looking teeth and regular features, men even remotely like Greek gods, are conscious of the surface they present and of its effect. They display themselves as if their faces are pictures already, finished, varnished, impermeable. Yvonne wants instead whatever it is that's behind the face and sees out through it. She chooses men who look as if things have happened to them, things they didn't like very much, men who show signs of the forces acting upon them, who have been chipped a little, rained on, frayed, like shells on the beach. A jaw slightly undershot, a nose too large or long, eyes of different sizes, asymmetry and counterpoise, these are the qualities that attract her. Men of this kind are not likely to be vain in any standard way. Instead they know that they must depend on something other than appearance to make an impact; but the mere act of being drawn throws them back upon their own unreliable bodies, their imperfect flesh. They watch her as she draws, puzzled, distrustful, yet at the same time vulnerable and oddly confiding. Something of theirs is in her hands.

Once Yvonne gets the men into her studio she is very delicate with them, very tactful. With them in mind she has purchased a second-hand armchair with a footstool to match: solid, comforting, wine velvet, not her usual taste. She sits them in it beside the large window, and turns them so that the light catches on their bones. She brings them a cup of tea or coffee, to put them at ease, and tells them how much she appreciates what they are doing for her. Her gratitude is real: she's about to eat their souls, not the whole soul of course, but even a small amount is not to be taken lightly. Sometimes she puts on a tape, something classical and not too noisy.

If she thinks they're relaxed enough she asks them to take off their shirts. She finds collar-bones very expressive, or rather the slight hollow at the V, the base of the throat; the wish-bone, which gives luck only when broken. The pulse there says something different from the pulse at wrist or temple. This is the place where, in historical movies set in mediaeval times, the arrow goes in.

When Yvonne has arranged her materials and started to draw, she goes quickly: for the sake of the men, she doesn't like to stretch things out. Having been subjected to it herself in her student days, when people posed for each other, she knows how excruciating it is to sit still and let yourself be looked at. The sound of the pencil travelling over the paper raises the small hairs on the skin, as if the pencil is not a pencil at all but a hand being passed over the body, half an inch from the surface. Not surprisingly, some of the men connect this sensation – which can be erotic – with Yvonne, and ask to take her out or see her again or even sleep with her.

Here Yvonne becomes fastidious. She asks if the man is married, and if he is, she asks if he's happy. She has no wish to get involved with an unhappily married man; she doesn't want to breathe anyone else's black smoke. But if he's happy, why would he want to sleep with her? If he isn't married, she thinks there must be some good reason why not. Mostly, when these invitations are issued, Yvonne refuses, gently and continuing to smile. She discounts protestations of love, passion, and undying friendship, praise of her beauty and talent, claims on her charity, whining, and bluster; she's heard these before. For Yvonne, only the simplest-minded rationale will do. 'Because I want to' is about all she'll accept.

Yvonne's studio is right downtown, near the waterfront, in an area of nineteenth-century factories and warehouses, some of which are still used in the original way, some of which have been taken over by people like her. In these streets there are drunks, derelicts, people who live in cardboard boxes; which doesn't bother Yvonne, since she hardly ever goes there at night. On the way to her studio in the mornings she has often passed a man who looks like Beethoven. He has the same domed forehead, overgrown brow bones, gloomy meditative scowl. His hair is grey and long and matted, and he wears a crumbling jeans suit and sneakers tied on with pieces of parcel string, even in winter, and carries a plastic-wrapped bundle that Yvonne thinks must contain everything he owns. He talks to himself and never looks at her. Yvonne would very much like to draw him, but he's far too crazy. She has a well-developed sense of self-protection, which must be why she hasn't landed in serious trouble with any of the men she picks up. This man alarms her, not because she thinks he's dangerous, but because he's a little too much like what she could become.

Nobody knows how old Yvonne is. She looks thirty and dresses as if she were twenty, though sometimes she looks forty and dresses as if she were fifty. Her age depends on the light, and what she wears depends on how she feels, which depends on how old she looks that day, which depends on the light. It's a delicate interaction. She wears her bronze-coloured hair cut short at the back and falling slantwise across her forehead, like Peter Pan's. Sometimes she rigs herself out in black leather pants and rides a very small motorcycle; on the other hand, sometimes she pins on a hat with a little veil, sticks a beauty mark on her cheek with an eyebrow pencil, and slings a secondhand silver fox with three tails around her neck.

She sometimes explains her age by saying she's old enough to remember garter belts when they were just ordinary articles of women's clothing. You wore them when you were young, before you were forced to put on girdles and become rubberized, like mothers. Yvonne remembers the advent of panty-hose, the death of the seamed stocking, whereas for younger women these events are only mythology.

She has another way of dating herself, which she uses less often. Once, when she was young but adult, she had a show of her paintings closed down by the police. It was charged with being obscene. She was one of the first artists in Toronto that this happened to. Just before that, no gallery would even have dared to mount the show, and shortly afterwards, when chains and blood and body parts in supermarket trays had become chic, it would have been considered tame. All Yvonne did at the time was to stick the penises onto men's bodies more or less the way they really were, and erect into the bargain. 'I don't see what the big deal was,' she can say, still ingenuously. 'I was only painting hard-ons. Isn't that what every man wants? The police were just jealous.' She goes on to add that she can't make out why, if a penis is a good thing, calling someone a penis-brain is an insult. She has this conversation only with people she knows very well or else has just met. The shocking thing about Yvonne, when she intends to be shocking, is the contrast between certain elements of her vocabulary and the rest of it, which, like her manner, is reserved and even secretive.

For a while she became a sort of celebrity, but that was because she was too inexperienced to know better. People made her into a cause, and even collected money for her, which was nice of them but got in the way, she now feels, of her reputation as a serious artist. It became boring to be referred to as 'the penis lady'. There was one advantage though: people bought her paintings, though not for ultra-top prices, especially after magic realism came back in. By this time she has money put away: she knows too much about the lives of artists to spend it all and have nothing to fall back on when the wind shifts and the crunch comes, though she sometimes worries that she'll be one of those old women found dead in a pile of empty cat-food cans with a million dollars stashed in her sock. She hasn't had a show now for several years; she calls it 'lying low'. The truth is she hasn't been producing much except her drawings of men. She has quite a few of them by now, but she isn't sure what she's going to do with them. Whatever she's looking for she hasn't yet found.

At the time of her revolutionary penises, she was more interested in bodies than she is now. Renoir was her hero, and she still admires him as a colourist, but she now finds his great lolloping nudes vapid and meaningless. Recently she's become obsessed with Holbein. A print of his portrait of Georg Gisze hangs in her bathroom, where she can see it while lying in the tub. Georg looks out at her, wearing a black fur coat and a wonderful pink silk shirt, each vein in his hands, each fingernail perfectly rendered, with a suggestion of darkness in his eyes, a wet shine on his lip, the symbols of his spiritual life around him. On his desk stands a vase, signifying the emptiness and vanity of mortal existence, with one carnation in it, signifying the Holy Ghost, or possibly betrothal. Earlier in her life Yvonne used to dismiss this kind of thing as the Rosemary for Remembrance school of flower arranging: everything had to mean something else. The thing about painting penises was that no one ever mistook them for phallic symbols, or indeed for symbols at all. But now she thinks it would be so handy if there were still some language of images like this, commonly known and understood. She would like to be able to put carnations between the fingers of the men she draws, but it's far too late for that. Surely Impressionism was a mistake, with its flesh that was merely flesh, however beautiful, its flowers that were merely flowers. (But what does she mean by 'merely'? Isn't that enough, for a flower to be itself? If Yvonne knew the answer . . .)

Yvonne likes to work in the late mornings, when the light is at its best in her studio. After that she sometimes has lunch, with various people she knows. She arranges these lunches from pay phones. She doesn't have a phone herself; when she did have one, she felt she was always at its mercy, whether it was ringing or not; mostly when it was not.

She doles out these lunches to herself like pills, at intervals, when she thinks she needs them. People living alone, she believes, get squirrelly if they go too long without human contact. Yvonne has had to learn how to take care of herself; she didn't always know. She's like a plant – not a sickly one, everybody comments on how healthy she always is – but a rare one, which can flourish and even live only under certain conditions. A transplant. She would like to write down instructions for herself and hand them over to someone else to be carried out, but despite several attempts on her part this hasn't proved to be possible.

She prefers small restaurants with tablecloths; the tablecloth gives her something to hold on to. She sits opposite whoever it is that day, her large green eyes looking out from behind the hair that keeps falling down over her forehead, her chin tilted so that the left side of her head is forward. She's convinced that she can hear better with her left ear than with her right, a belief that has nothing to do with deafness.

Her friends enjoy having lunch with Yvonne, though probably they wouldn't enjoy it as much if they did it more often. They would find themselves running out of things to say. As it is, Yvonne is a good listener: she's always so interested in everything. (There's no deception here: she is interested in everything, in a way.) She likes to catch up on what people are doing. Nobody gets around to catching up on what she is doing, because she gives the impression of being so serene, so perfectly balanced, that their minds are at rest about her. Whatever she's doing is so obviously the right thing. When they do ask, she has a repertoire of anecdotes about herself which are amusing but not very informative. When she runs out of these, she tells jokes. She writes down the punch lines and keeps them on filing cards in her purse so she won't forget them.

She eats out alone, but not often. When she does, it's usually at sushi bars, where she can sit with her back to the rest of the room and watch the hands of the chefs as they deftly caress and stroke her food. As she eats, she can almost feel their fingers in her mouth.

Yvonne lives on the top floor of a large house in an older but newly stylish part of the city. She has two big rooms, a bathroom, a kitchenette concealed by louvred folding doors which she keeps closed most of the time, and a walk-out deck on which there are several planters made from barrels sawed in two. These once contained rose-bushes, not Yvonne's. This floor used to be the attic, and although Yvonne has to go through the rest of the house to get to it, there's a door at the bottom of her stairs that she can lock if she wants to.

The house is owned by a youngish couple named Al and Judy, who both work for the town planning department of City Hall and are full of talk and projects. They intend to expand their own living area into Yvonne's floor when their mortgage is paid off; it will be a study for Al. Meanwhile, they are delighted to have a tenant like Yvonne. These arrangements are so fragile, so open to incompatibility and other forms of disaster, so easily destroyed by stereo sets and mud on the rugs. But Yvonne is a gem, says Judy: they never hear a peep out of her. She's almost too quiet for Al, who would rather hear the footsteps when someone comes up behind him. He refers to Yvonne as 'The Shadow,' but only when he's had a hard day at work and a couple of drinks.

Anyway, the advantages far outweigh the disadvantages. Al and Judy have a year-old baby named Kimberly, who is at day-care in the mornings and Judy's office in the afternoons, but if they want to go out in the evenings and Yvonne is in, they have no hesitation about leaving Kimberly in her charge. They don't ask her to put Kimberly to bed herself, however. They have never said she's just like one of the family; they don't make that mistake. Sometimes Yvonne comes down and sits in the kitchen while Kimberly is being fed, and Judy thinks she can spot a wistful expression in Yvonne's eyes.

At night when they're lying in bed or in the morning when

they're getting dressed, Al and Judy sometimes talk about Yvonne. Each has a different version of her, based on the fact that she never has men over, or even women. Judy thinks she has no sex life at all; she's given it up, for a reason which is probably tragic. Al thinks she does have a sex life, but carries it on elsewhere. A woman who looks like Yvonne – he's not specific – has to be getting it somehow. Judy says he's a dirty old man, and pokes him in the midriff.

'Who knows what evil lurks in the hearts of men?' Al says. 'Yvonne knows.'

As for Yvonne, the situation suits her, for now. She finds it comforting to hear the sounds of family life going on beneath her, especially in the evenings, and when she goes away Judy waters her plants. She doesn't have many of these. In fact, she doesn't have much of anything, in Judy's opinion: an architectural drawing board, a rug and some cushions and a low table, a couple of framed prints, and, in the bedroom, two futons, one on top of the other. Judy speculated at first that the second was for when some man slept over, but none ever does. Yvonne's place is always very tidy, but to Judy it looks precarious. It's too portable, she feels, as if the whole establishment could be folded up in a minute and transported and unfolded almost anywhere else. Judy tells Al that she wouldn't be surprised one morning to find that Yvonne had simply vanished. Al tells her not to be silly: Yvonne is responsible, she'd never go without giving notice. Judy says she's talking about a feeling, not about what she thinks objectively is really going to happen. Al is always so literal.

Al and Judy have two cats, which are very curious about Yvonne. They climb up to her deck and meow at the french doors to be let in. If she leaves her door ajar, they are up her stairs like a shot. Yvonne has no objection to them, except when they jump on her head while she's resting. Sometimes she will pick up one of them and hold it so that its paws are on either side of her neck and she can feel its heart beating against her. The cats find this position uncomfortable.

Once in a while Yvonne disappears for days, maybe even a week at a time. Al and Judy don't worry about her, since she says when she'll be back and she's always there at the time stated. She never tells them where she's going, but she leaves a sealed envelope with them which she claims contains instructions for how she could be reached in case of an emergency. She doesn't say what would constitute an emergency. Judy sticks the envelope carefully behind the wall telephone in the kitchen; she doesn't know it's empty.

Al and Judy have incorporated these absences of Yvonne's into the romances they have built up about her. In Al's, she's off to meet a lover, whose identity must remain secret, either because he's married or for reasons of state, or both. He imagines this lover as much richer and more important than he is. For Judy, Yvonne is visiting the child or children Judy is convinced she has. The father is a brute, and more strong-willed than Yvonne, who anyone can see is the kind of woman who couldn't stand up to either physical violence or a long court battle. This is the only thing that can excuse, for Judy, Yvonne's abandonment of her children. Yvonne is allowed to see them only at infrequent intervals. Judy pictures her meeting them in restaurants, in parks, the constraint, the anguish of separation. She spoons applesauce into the wet pink oyster-like mouth of Kimberly and bursts into tears.

'Don't be silly,' says Al. 'She's just off having a roll in the hay. It'll do her a world of good.' Al thinks Yvonne has been looking too pale.

'You think sex with a man is the big solution to everything, don't you?' says Judy, wiping her eyes with the sleeve of her sweater.

Al pats her. 'Not the only one,' he says, 'but it's better than a slap with a wet noodle, eh?'

Sometimes it is a slap with a wet noodle, thinks Judy, who has been over-tired recently and feels too many demands are being made upon her. But she smiles up at Al with fondness and appreciation. She knows she's lucky. The standard against which she measures her luck is Yvonne.

Thus the existence of Yvonne and her slightly weird behaviour lead to marital communication and eventual concord. If she knew this, Yvonne would be both pleased and a little scornful; but deep down underneath she would not give a piss.

When everything has been smooth and without painful incident for some time, when the tide has gone out too far, when Yvonne has been wandering along the street, looking with curiosity but no great interest at the lighting fixtures, the coral-encrusted bottles and the bridesmaids' dresses, the waterlogged shoes and the antique candle-holders held up by winged nymphs and the gasping fish that the receding waters have left glistening and exposed in all their detail, when she's gone into the Donut Centre and sat down at the counter and seen the doughnuts under glass beneath her elbows, their tentacles drawn in, breathing lightly, every grain of sugar distinct, she knows that up on the hills, in the large suburban yards, the snakes and moles are coming out of their burrows and the earth is trembling imperceptibly beneath the feet of the old men in cardigans and tweed caps raking their lawns. She gets up and goes out, no faster than usual and not forgetting to leave a tip. She's considerate of waitresses because she never wants to be one again.

She heads for home, trying not to hurry. Behind her, visible over her shoulder if she would only turn her head, and approaching with horrifying but silent speed, is a towering wall of black water. It catches the light of the sun, there are glints of movement, of life caught up in it and doomed, near its translucent crest.

Yvonne climbs the stairs to her apartment, almost running, the two cats bounding up behind her, and hits the bed just as the blackness breaks over her head with a force that tears the pillow out of her hands and blinds and deafens her. Confusion sweeps over and around her, but underneath the surface terror she is not too frightened. She's done this before, she has some trust in the water, she knows that all she has to do is draw her knees up and close everything, ears, eyes, mouth, hands. All she has to do is hold on. Some would advocate that she let go instead, ride with the current, but she's tried it. Collision with other floating objects does her no good. The cats jump on her head, walk on her, purr in her ear; she can hear them in the distance, like flute music on a hillside, up on the shore.

Yvonne can think of no reason for these episodes. There's no trigger for them, no early warning. They're just something that happens to her, like a sneeze. She thinks of them as chemical.

Today Yvonne is having lunch with a man whose collar-bone she admires, or did admire when it was available to her. Right now it isn't, because Yvonne is no longer sleeping with this man. She stopped because of the impossibility of the situation. For Yvonne, situations become impossible quickly. She doesn't like situations.

This is a man with whom Yvonne was once in love. There are several such men in Yvonne's life; she makes a distinction between them and the men she draws. She never draws men she's in love with; she thinks it's because she lacks the necessary distance from them. She sees them, not as form or line or colour or even expression, but as concentrations of the light. (That's her version of it when she's in love; when she isn't, she remembers them as rarified blurs, like something you've spilled on a table-cloth and are trying to wash out. She has occasionally made the mistake of trying to explain all this to the men concerned.) She's no stranger to addiction, having once passed far too many chemical travelogues through her body, and she knows its dangers. As far as she's concerned love is just another form of it.

She can't stand too much of this sort of thing, so her affairs with such men don't last long. She doesn't begin them with any illusions about permanence, or even about temporary domestic arrangements; the days are gone when she could believe that if only she could climb into bed with a man and pull the covers over both their heads, they would be safe.

However, she often likes these men and thinks that something is due them, and so she continues to see them afterwards, which is easy because her separations from them are never unpleasant, not any more. Life is too short.

Yvonne sits across from the man, at a table in a small restaurant, holding on to the tablecloth with one hand, below the table where he can't see it. She's listening to him with her customary interest, head tilted. She misses him intensely; or rather, she misses, not him, but the sensations he used to be able to arouse in her. The light has gone out of him and now she can see him clearly. She finds this objectivity of hers, this clarity, almost more depressing than she can bear, not because there is anything hideous or repellant about this man but because he has now returned to the ordinary level, the level of things she can see, in all their amazing and complex particularity, but cannot touch.

He's come to the end of what he's been saying, which had to do with politics. Now it's time for Yvonne to tell him a joke.

'Why is pubic hair curly?' she says.

'Why?' he says; as usual, he attempts to conceal the shock he feels at hearing her say words like *pubic*. Nice men are more difficult for Yvonne than pigs. If a man is piggish enough, she's glad to see him go.

'So you won't poke your eyes out,' says Yvonne, clutching the tablecloth.

Instead of laughing he smiles at her, a little sadly. 'I don't know how you do it,' he says. 'Nothing ever bothers you.'

Yvonne pauses. Maybe he's referring to the fact that, in their withdrawal from each other, there were no frantic phone calls from her, no broken dishes, no accusations, no tears. She's tried all these in the past and found them lacking. But maybe he wanted those things, as proof of something, of love perhaps; maybe he's disappointed by her failure to provide them.

'Things bother me,' says Yvonne.

'You have so much energy,' he goes on, as if he hasn't heard her. 'Where do you get it from? What's your secret?'

Yvonne looks down at her plate, on which there is half an

apple and walnut and watercress salad and a crust of bread. To touch his hand, which is there in plain view, on the tablecloth a mere six inches away from her wine glass, would be to put herself at risk again, and she is already at risk. Once she delighted in being at risk; but once she did everything too much.

She looks up at him and smiles. 'My secret is that I get up every morning to watch the sunrise,' she says. This *is* her secret, though it's not the only one; it's only the one that's on offer today. She watches him to see if he's bought it, and he has. This is enough in character for him, it's what he thinks she's really like. He's satisfied that she's all right, that there will be no trouble, which is what he wanted to know. He orders another cup of coffee and asks for the bill. When it comes, Yvonne pays half.

They walk out into the March air, warmer than usual this year, a fact on which they both comment. Yvonne avoids shaking hands with him. It occurs to her that he is the last man she will ever have the energy to love. It's so much work. He waves good-bye to her and gets onto a streetcar and is borne away, towards a set of distant stoplights, along tracks that converge as they recede.

Near the streetcar stop there's a small flower shop where you can buy one flower at a time, if one flower is all you want. It's all Yvonne ever wants. Today they have tulips, for the first time this year, and Yvonne chooses a red one, the inside of the cup an acrylic orange. She will take this tulip back to her room and set it in a white bud vase in the sunlight and drink its blood until it dies.

Yvonne carries the tulip in one hand, wrapped in its cone of paper, held stiffly out in front of her as if it's dripping. Walking along past the store windows, into which she peers with her usual eagerness, her usual sense that maybe, today, she will discover behind them something that will truly be worth seeing, she feels as if her feet are not on cement at all but on ice. The blade of the skate floats, she knows, on a thin film of water, which it melts by pressure and which freezes behind it. This is the freedom of the present tense, this sliding edge.

Yvonne is drawing another man. As a rule, she draws only men who fall well within the norm: they dress more or less conventionally, they turn out, when asked, to have jobs recognized and respected by society, they're within ten years of her own age, shooting either way. This one is different.

She began to follow him about three blocks past the flower shop, trotting along behind him – he has long legs – with her tulip held up in front of her like a child's flag. He's young, maybe twenty-three, and on the street he was carrying a black leather portfolio, which is now leaning against the wall by her door. His pants were black leather too, and his jacket, under which he was wearing a hot-pink shirt. His head is shaved up the back and sides, leaving a plume on top, dyed fake-fur orang-outang orange, and he has two gold earrings in his left ear. The leather portfolio means that he's an artist or a designer of some sort; she suspects he's a spray-painter, the kind that goes around at night and writes things on brick walls, things like *crunchy granola sucks* and *Save Soviet Jews! Win Big Prizes!* If he ever draws at all, it's with pink and green fluorescent felt pens. She'd bet ten dollars he can't draw fingers. Yvonne's own renderings of fingers are very good.

In the past she's avoided anything that looked like another artist, but there's something about him, the sullenness, the stylistic belligerence, the aggressive pastiness and deliberate potato-sprouting-in-the-cellar lack of health. When she caught sight of him, Yvonne felt a shock of recognition, as if this was what she'd been looking for, though she doesn't yet know why. She ran him to earth outside a submarine shop and said her piece. She expected a rejection, rude at that, but here he is, in her studio, wearing nothing at the moment but his pink shirt, one bloodless leg thrown over the arm of the wine velvet chair. In his hand is the tulip, which clashes violently with the shirt and the chair and his hair, which all clash with each other. He's like a welding-shop accident, a motorcycle driven full tilt into a cement wall. The look he's focussing on her is pure defiance, but defiance of what? She doesn't know why he agreed to come with her. All he said was, 'Sure, why not?' with a look she read as meaning that she totally failed to impress him.

Yvonne draws, her pencil moving lightly over his body. She knows she has to go quickly or he will get restless, he will escape her. She can put the tulip in later, when she paints him. Already she's decided to paint him; he will be her first real painting for years. The tulip will become a poppy; it's almost the right colour anyway.

She's only down to the collar-bone, half visible under the open shirt, when he says, 'That's enough,' and pulls himself out of the chair and comes over and stands behind her. He puts his hands on her waist and presses himself against her: no preliminaries here, which would suit Yvonne fine – she likes these things to be fast – except that she's uneasy about him. None of her usual mollifications, coffee, music, gratefulness, have worked on him: he's maintained a consistent level of surliness. He's beyond her. She thinks of Al and Judy's cat, the black one, and the time it got its foot caught in the cord of her Venetian blind. It was so enraged she had to throw a towel over it to get it untangled.

'That's *art*,' he says, looking over her shoulder.

Yvonne mistakes this for a compliment, until he says, 'Art sucks.' There's a hiss in the last word.

Yvonne gasps: there is such hatred in his voice. Maybe if she just stands there nothing will happen. He turns away from her and goes to the corner near the door: he wants to show her what he's got in his portfolio. What he does are collages. The settings are all outdoors: woods, meadows, rocks, seashores. Onto them he has pasted women, meticulously cut from magazines, splayed openlegged torsoes with the hands and feet removed, sometimes the heads, over-painted with nail polish in various shades of purple and red, shiny and wet-looking against the paper.

Yet as a lover he is slow and meditative, abstracted, somnambulent almost, as if the motions he's going through are only a kind of afterthought, like a dog groaning in a dream. The violence is all on the cardboard; it's only art, after all. Maybe everything is only art, Yvonne thinks, picking her sky-blue shirt up off the floor, buttoning it. She wonders how many times in the future she will find herself doing up these particular buttons.

When he's gone out, she locks the door behind him and sits in the red velvet chair. It's herself she's in danger from. She decides to go away for a week. When she comes back she will buy a canvas the size of a doorway and begin again. Though if art sucks and everything is only art, what has she done with her life?

In her medicine cabinet Yvonne keeps several bottles of pills, which she has collected from doctors on one pretext or another over the years. There was no need to do this, to go through the rigmarole of prescriptions, since anything you want is available on the street and Yvonne knows who from; yet the prescriptions gave her a kind of sanction. Even the actual pieces of paper, with their illegible Arabic-textured scrawls, reassured her, much as a charm would if she believed in them.

At one time she knew exactly how many pills to take, of which kinds, at which precisely timed intervals, to keep from either throwing up or passing out before the right dose had been reached. She knew what she would say ahead of time to fend off those who might otherwise come looking for her, where she would go, which doors she would lock, where and in what position she would lie down; even, and not least importantly, what she would wear. She wanted her body to look well and not be too troublesome to those who would eventually have to deal with it. Clothed corpses are so much less disturbing than naked ones.

But lately she's been forgetting much of this arcane knowledge. She should throw the pills out: they've become obsolete. She's replaced them with something much simpler, more direct, faster, more failure-proof, and, she's been told, less painful. A bathtub full of warm water, her own bathtub in the bathroom she uses every day, and an ordinary razor blade, for which no prescriptions are necessary. The recommendation is that the lights be turned out, to avoid panic: if you can't see the spreading red, you hardly know it's there. A stinging at the wrists, like a minor insect. She pictures herself wearing a flannel nightgown, printed with small pink flowers, that buttons up to the neck. She has not yet bought this.

She keeps a razor blade in her paintbox; it could be for slicing paper. In fact she does slice paper with it, and when it gets dull she replaces it. One side of the blade is taped, since she has no desire to cut her fingers by accident.

Yvonne hardly ever thinks about this razor blade and what it's really doing in her paintbox. She is not obsessed with death, her own or anybody else's. She doesn't approve of suicide; she finds it morally distasteful. She takes care crossing the street, watches what she puts into her mouth, saves her money.

But the razor blade is there all the time, underneath everything. Yvonne needs it there. What it means is that she can control her death; and if she can't do that, what control can she ever possibly achieve over her life?

Perhaps the razor blade is only a kind of *memento mori*, after all. Perhaps it's only a pictorial flirtation. Perhaps it's only a dutiful symbol, like the carnation on the desk of Holbein's young man. He isn't looking at the carnation anyway, he's looking out of the picture, so earnestly, so intently, so sweetly. He's looking at Yvonne, and he can see in the dark.

The days are getting longer, and Yvonne's alarm clock goes off earlier and earlier. In the summers she takes to having afternoon naps, to make up for the sleep she loses to these dawn rituals. She hasn't missed the sunrise for years; she depends on it. It's almost as if she believes that if she isn't there to see it there will be no sunrise at all.

And yet she knows that her dependence is not on something that can be grasped, held in the hand, kept, but only on an accident of the language, because *sunrise* should not be a noun. The sunrise is not a thing, but only an effect of the light caused by the positions of two astronomical bodies in relation to each other. The sun does not really rise at all, it's the earth that turns. The sunrise is a fraud.

Today there's no overcast. Yvonne, standing out on her deck in her too-thin Japanese robe, holds on to the wooden railing to keep from lifting her arms as the sun floats up above the horizon, like a shimmering white blimp, an enormous kite whose string she almost holds in her hand. Light, chilly and thin but light, reaches her from it. She breathes it in.

From *Bluebeard's Egg and Other Stories*, published by Virago.

The Bishop's Lunch

....
MICHÈLE ROBERTS

THE ANGEL of the resurrection has very long wings. Their tips
end in single quills. The angel of the resurrection has three pairs
of wings that swaddle him in black shawls then unwrap when he
needs them, nervous and strong. The angel of the resurrection
flies in the darkness. He is invisible and black. His feathers are
soft as black fur.

That is what Sister Josephine of the Holy Face was thinking
early on that Wednesday morning of Holy Week four days before
Easter. Uncertain whether or not her picture of the angel was
theologically sound, she decided that she would record it later
on in her little black notebook, the place where she was required
to write down all her faults. These were confessed at a weekly
interview with the Novice Mistress and were then atoned for by
suitable penances. The little black notebook was one of the few
items Sister Josephine had been allowed to bring with her from
home when she entered the convent seven months previously.
Her mother had put it in her suitcase herself, along with a new
missal and four pairs of black woollen stockings.

A thought which Sister Josephine of the Holy Face knew she
would not write down in the little book was that she ought to
be called Sister Josephine of the Unholy Stomach. At home on
the farm eight kilometres inland from Etretat she had drunk her
breakfast *café au lait* from a china bowl stencilled with blue
flowers. She had eaten warm crusty bread fetched half an hour
before from the village bakery. On Sundays there was hot chocolate after High Mass, with brioche or galette, and a hearty

appetite seen as a good thing. Here in the convent on the outskirts of Rouen the day-old bread was always stale, and the thin coffee bitter with chicory and drunk from a tin cup.

Angels, having no bodies, were not tormented by memories of *saucisson* and cold fresh butter, of thick sourish cream poured over cod and potatoes, over beans, over artichokes. Yet the black feathers of the wings of the angel of the resurrection were very soft.

Sister Josephine was down on her hands and knees in front of the cupboard under the big stone sink of the convent kitchen, groping inside it for the bread-knife she had unaccountably mislaid. Her fingers closed over a bunch of silky plumage. It wasn't an angel's wing, she discovered when she brought it out, but the feather duster she had lost a month ago. Her penance for that had been to kiss the ground in the refectory before breakfast every day for a week. The taste of floor polish. She shivered as she remembered it.

The bell rang for chapel. Sister Josephine spotted the bread-knife hiding behind a bucket of washing soda. Squatting back on her haunches, she flung it, with the feather duster, on to the wooden table behind her. Then she straightened up, untied the strings of her heavy blue cotton apron, and hung it on the nail behind the door. Not *my* apron, she reminded herself: *ours*.

She glided along the dark cloister as rapidly as she dared. She wasn't supposed to begin her kitchen duties so early, but she'd wanted to get on with slicing up the long baguettes into the bread-baskets ready for breakfast. There was too much work in the kitchen for one person to do, even in such a small community, but to complain would be a sin against obedience. Putting Sister Josephine in sole charge of the cooking, the Novice Mistress had announced six weeks earlier, was a real test of her faith. And of the nun's digestions, Sister Josephine had muttered to herself.

She knelt in her stall, amongst the other novices, yawning as she tried to follow the still unfamiliar Latin psalms. Her empty stomach growled, and she clasped her hands more tightly together. They were chilblained, and smelt of carbolic soap. Now they looked like her mother's hands: red, roughened by work. Her mother's hands were capable, quick and deft for the labour of farmyard and house. They were expert at cooking, too. She was famous among the village women for the lightness of her choux pastry, the *gougères* and eclairs she turned out on feast-days. Sister Josephine had resisted all her mother's attempts to teach her the domestic arts. She had refused to believe that God wanted her to serve Him through topping and tailing beans, peeling potatoes. She'd hungered for transcendence, for the ecstasy of mystical union. She hadn't come to the convent to *cook*.

What in heaven, Sister Josephine asked herself for perhaps the hundredth time that Lent, am I going to do about the Bishop's lunch?

It was an ancient tradition in the convent that every year on Easter Sunday the Bishop of the diocese would say High Mass in the convent chapel and then join Reverend Mother, the Novice Mistress and the other senior nuns at their table in the refectory for the midday meal. To celebrate the end of the rigorous fasting of Lent and the presence of such a distinguished guest, and, of course, the resurrection of the Saviour from the dead, an elegant array of dishes was always served. Sister Josephine knew that the Bishop, like all holy men of the cloth, had renounced the pleasures of the flesh, but she knew too that nonetheless he would expect to be given exquisite food just so that he could demonstrate his indifference to it as he ate.

Help me, she prayed: please help me.

Normally she did not bother God with problems over lost feather dusters and bread-knives and how to turn a few cabbages and turnips into a nourishing soup for twenty hungry nuns. God, being male, was above such trivia. But the Bishop's lunch was an emergency. It was better to bypass Our Lady and the saints this time, to go straight to the top.

The smell of incense, pungent and sweet, made her open her eyes. Morning Mass had begun and she hadn't even noticed. Daydreaming again. Another fault to note down in her little black book. Sighing, she reached into the skirt pocket of her habit, drew it out, and opened it hastily at random. Her stubby black pencil hovered over the page. She drew in a sharp quick breath, and then released it.

Maundy Thursday passed peacefully, apart from the gardener mentioning to Reverend Mother that someone had taken his old and rusty rifle from its usual place in the shed, and that someone else had thoughtfully weeded all the wild sorrel from under the apple trees in the orchard.

On Good Friday the gardener told Reverend Mother he'd heard rifle shots coming from the field backing on to the kitchen garden. Also, the traps he'd laid for rabbits, all three of them, had been sprung by some poacher. And when he went to investigate a great squawking in the chicken shed, he found that the best layers among the hens had been robbed of all their eggs. There would be none to take to market the following week.

Reverend Mother sighed. She was getting old, and tired, and did not want to be faced with all these practical problems. She consoled the gardener as best she could. Then she sent for Sister Josephine. How, she enquired of the young novice, was she going to manage to make a lunch on Easter Sunday fit for a Bishop to eat? Well, Sister Josephine explained: I have been praying for a miracle.

All through that Good Friday afternoon the nuns knelt in the gloomy chapel, all its statues shrouded in purple and its candles extinguished, following the Passion of the Saviour as he was stripped and scourged, crowned with thorns, and then forced to carry his heavy cross up the hill to Calvary. Finally, he was nailed to the cross, and hung from it. The nuns sang the great dialogues of the Church, taken from the Old Testament, between Christ and his God, Christ and his people. *My people, what have you done to me? Answer me.* Rain beat at the chapel windows. Christ cried out for the last time and then died. The nuns filed from the chapel, ate their frugal supper, the only meal of the day.

On Holy Saturday Christ was in the tomb and Sister Josephine was in the kitchen. Swathed in her blue apron, she scrubbed the sink, the table, the floor. Then, on the table, she laid out certain items from her *batterie de cuisine*: a wooden spoon, an egg whisk, several long, very sharp knives.

The rabbits she had taken from the gardener's traps were hanging in the pantry. Swiftly she skinned them, one by one, then cut them up and threw them into a pot with a bunch of herbs and half a bottle of communion wine. Next she fetched the pigeons she had shot two days earlier, plucked and trussed them, and arranged them on a bed of apples in a well-buttered dish. Finally she prepared a small mountain of potatoes and leeks, washed a big bunch of sorrel and patted it dry in a cloth, and checked that the two dozen eggs she had removed from the hens were safe in their wicker basket in the store-room.

When the knock came on the back door of the kitchen she was ready. Opening it, she smiled at the boy who stood there, at the silvery aluminium churn and squat bottle he clasped in his arms. The boy's eyes were as blue as hers, his nose as aquiline, his chin as determined. They kissed each other on both cheeks. Sister Josephine took the churn and the bottle, smiled at the boy again, and shut the door on him. Now everything was as ready for tomorrow as it could be.

Very early next morning, just before dawn, the nuns gathered outside the chapel to see the New Fire lit in the cold windy courtyard. Now the great candle, symbol of the risen Christ, could blaze in the darkness. Easter Sunday had arrived. Now the chapel could be filled with flowers and lights, the dark coverings taken off the statues, and the altars hung with lace and white brocade.

The Bishop, with his retinue, arrived to say High Mass. The organ pealed, the nuns stood up very straight in their stalls and sang a loud psalm of praise: Christ is risen, Christ is risen, alleluia.

This miracle of the Resurrection was repeated in the Mass: through the actions of his chosen one, his priest, Christ offered his body, his blood, to nourish his faithful children. The Bishop's hands moved deftly amongst his holy cutlery. He wiped the chalice, picked up the silver cruets of water and wine, attended to the incense boat. Alleluia, sang the nuns: Christ has leapt from the tomb. Meanwhile, in the kitchen, Sister Josephine's choux pastry leapt in the oven.

The Bishop's lunch, all the nuns later agreed, was a great and unexpected success. The rabbit pâté, scented with juniper, was exquisite. So too was the dish of roasted pigeons with apples and calvados, the sliced potatoes and leeks baked in cream, the poached eggs in sorrel sauce. But, they unanimously declared, the *pièce de résistance* of the entire banquet was the creation which ended it: the figure of an angel sculpted from choux buns stuck together with caramel and then coated with dark bitter-chocolate cream. His arms were held out wide, and his three pairs of black wings extended behind him. A very noble confection, said the nuns: truly, a miracle.

After finishing the washing-up, Sister Josephine went upstairs to her curtained cell in the novices' dormitory. This was forbidden in the daytime, but she didn't care. She sat on her bed and took out her little black book. She opened it, and leafed through the recipes so carefully written out in her mother's handwriting in its centre pages. Perhaps, Sister Josephine thought, my vocation is to leave the convent, train as a chef, and open my own restaurant.

From *During Mother's Absence*, published by Virago.

Grizzly Mountain

BONNIE BURNARD

SHE WAS to leave on Monday. He would help her pack and carry her bag down to the hotel. He would load her into the beat-up station wagon that took people into the city and close the door on her, likely carefully and without much force. He said it was right that she should go through the physical act of removing herself from him. He said it would help if she could put a distance between them, said it was healthy. He had already put his distance there.

But he said they might as well go on Saturday's climb as planned, as promised. The exertion would be a cleansing. She allowed him these pronouncements because she knew she would think of him for a long time and it would be useful to think of him sometimes as a pompous ass.

They had lived in the small mountain town for almost two years. It was a poor town but so isolated that those who lived there were allowed to forget their poverty most of the time. The people had no compelling past, talked not about themselves as they sat in the hotel beer parlour but about the ones who had deserted when the mine shut down years before and about the ones who had drifted in and out of town since. He was there to teach their kids in the prosperous looking old school; she was there to be with him.

They had climbed the mountain before, in the winter. They'd had cross-country skis and good boots to change into when they'd had to leave the skis behind at the base of the mountain. It had been fine between them then. He smiled whenever he

48

looked at her on that climb, his face seemed to take the smile from her and hold it after he turned away. She knew she was strong and beautiful. Now that he didn't find his smiles in her, she felt something less than strong, something less than beautiful.

The boy had been promised the climb. He was one of the man's students, a small tight boy with beige hair and beige skin and eyes as blue as the lakes that could be seen from the top of the mountain, after the climb. And he had shadows drifting across his eyes, like the clouds drifting in reflection across the lakes.

The boy worshipped the man. It was good clean worship, full of imitation and quick grins. The boy's father had been one of the men who had left the town when the mine closed. He had neither returned nor sent for his family. The boy didn't speak of his absent father and she suspected it was because he had learned, quite bravely, to live with the unspeakable. She often thought when she looked at him that she could kill a man who left a child. A man who could turn his back on that kind of love had nothing to do with life. A man like that was an aberration.

It took no particular effort to include the boy in their lives; he was just quietly there with them, leaving at night to go to his bed as a child of their own might have done. He hadn't been told that she was leaving. He would know on Monday. She thought maybe her leaving would clear some space for him around the man, maybe even please him. There was certainly no need to exclude him from this last climb. Nothing meaningful would be said. She knew the danger of trying to say things for the sake of memory. There would be no closing ceremony.

They packed their gear the night before the climb, packed the food in the morning, after breakfast. They would have cheese and salami and molasses bread for lunch and cold chicken later in the evening, at the fire. And wine, though it made her sneeze. It was one of the things that got under his skin, her sneezing over a glass of fine wine. They often took some with them on small hikes out to one of the lakes where they could be alone, where they could claim all the space around them, miles of it.

He needed that much space and he loved the wine then. The sneezing had overtaken her on one of their first hikes, with the Riesling, he'd looked aghast, said it was like farting in a cathedral. She had no particular respect for cathedrals. In retrospect, she began to recognize his comment as the sign that there would be things about her which he would not forgive.

But he was a good friend to her in their sagging bed and on the mountain wildflowers and on the stony beaches. He said she was the space he needed, she was distance, said he could be in her without being aware of her breath on his neck. She didn't care about definition, only hoped she could always be distance, if that was what he loved.

When it was time to set out in the morning, the boy was at their door with his packsack, ready. He offered no hints of manhood. He was graceful and confident, had not yet begun to stretch and stumble. She had seen him swim nude many times and he was hairless, his skin innocent and fresh in the sun. And he took her own nudity with just a slight puzzlement. She was confident she did not exist in his dreams.

He helped her fasten her packsack, gave the man a fake punch on the shoulder and they started out away from the town. When they were nearly at the end of the main street, where the wild country took immediate control, the man who ran the coffee shop waved and hailed them, quickly put a half dozen warm cinnamon buns in a bag and gave it to them, as he had on other mornings when they were setting out. He had been a friend of the boy's father, years before.

They didn't talk as they walked, even the boy didn't need talk. They went quietly deeper into the wild landscape, the distance. Before her time with him, it would not have seemed like distance at all. Distance was uninterrupted, immeasurable, it was snow blankets tucked securely across the prairie, the mildest curve of hills almost immodest. This place was unsettled, flamboyant. The land seemed actually to move as you watched it. It climbed uncontrolled toward the clouds, climbed till it was clear of the trees, threw itself over the top of mountains, eager for valleys. It split itself into streams at their feet, gathered together again to hold arrangements of wildflowers and scrub.

The boy sometimes went on ahead of them, blazing a new trail with the hatchet the man had given him for his eighth birthday. Sometimes he strayed behind them. She sensed he did this so he could have them framed against the dark growth through which they were climbing, as in a picture. Occasionally he would hustle up to her if there were rocks to manage or a stream to jump across, would take her hand in his small one, like an escort.

They were two hours reaching the top of the mountain and they were greeted by deer scrambling over the far edge, giving up their territory, as they always did. The deer would be back, though they would not come close.

The three of them set up camp together, establishing a place for the fire, putting their sleeping bags out, three in a row, gathering twigs and dead grass. They would go back down the side later to collect wood for the fire. She broke open the food pack and started to slice cheese and meat with the fine cool blade of the hunting knife, which the man carried in its sheath on his belt. He'd bought the knife as a present for himself with his first paycheque. He'd come back from shopping with the knife and a shawl for her. The shawl was creamy white with mauve and blue threads woven into the edging. He'd wrapped it around her shoulders and slipped his knife over his belt and they'd sat quietly together in front of a fire.

He had been right about the exercise of the climb. She had forgotten for all that time that she was leaving on Monday. Here at the top of the mountain, eating bread and cheese and meat, she remembered. She thought that if the boy hadn't come, if they had been alone, she might have tried to create a final afternoon. But such a final afternoon would have held chaotic words like sorry and maybe and impossibility. Such a final afternoon would have been like this landscape. She held herself flat and silent, allowed no movement, no shadows. It took all her energy to keep the calm in force.

The man and the boy played chase. They ran over to the small lake near the far edge and threw themselves on the grass, rolling over and over, yelling and laughing, uninhibited, free of all restraint but gravity. She knew they would leap off the mountain without hesitation if not for that one unavoidable pull.

They returned to her and they all slept for a while, together in their row of sleeping bags, and when they awoke the deer were back, grazing. The deer stayed this time and the boy began to talk. He talked of an uncle who had a farm in the south of the province and of another who'd once had a fishing boat. They moved from the uncles to other people, the boy anxious to be told of other kinds of lives, other kinds of towns and landscapes. They took him across the Prairies and up across the Shield, around Lake Superior and down into the south where so many people lived, and through Quebec, through maple sugar bushes and small farms, on through the eastern provinces where they tried to imitate for him the way people talked. He laughed hard at their efforts, threw his head back and held his stomach and she wanted to hug him tight to her own. They took him to that other coast with its steep cliffs and its deadly ocean.

And the man took him to England while she prepared their supper, dividing the chicken evenly among them. The boy very quietly, without taking his eyes off the man's face, got a bag out of his pack. In the bag were three chocolate bars and a package of squashed potato chips. She divided the chips, arranging them beside the chicken with the care of a dinner party hostess.

The boy looked at the plates with pride then and gave her one of his best quick grins. He asked if she wanted more wood for the fire and sprinted down over the side to get it. In the boy's absence, the man knelt behind her and put his hand on her back, rubbing the ridges of her spine through her sweater. He lifted her hair and put the cold tip of his nose behind her ear, his teeth on the back of her neck. She continued to divide and arrange, separate and rearrange. When a shudder twisted down her spine, he lifted his mouth.

After supper they talked of more countries, sharing with the boy all the information they could summon, all they knew about places they'd been and hadn't been. On the return trip he led them, checking his facts as he brought them country by country, province by province, back to the fire on the top of the mountain. He said he didn't think he'd like the Prairies much and it made her catch her breath, made her concentrate for a tough minute on holding a placid face.

When the fire went out they stripped down to their underwear and settled into the sleeping bags, leaving the tops unzipped, loose over them. The night air was gently cool. She lay facing the man for a few minutes and he stroked her hair, tried to rub the creases out of her forehead. He said she'd be happier. He made no effort to keep the love out of his eyes and so, enraged, she turned to face the sky. Stars and light won out against the dark space, making it seem more distant than it really was. She turned again then, toward the boy, who was quiet beside her, his breathing regular and peaceful. She turned finally to the distance within her, turned to it for help against the need to fight, the need to stay. She grieved without sound for most of the night. The man did not try to save her from it.

In the morning she woke to the smell of smoke from the breakfast fire and to an overwhelming sense of love being offered. When she came fully awake she recognized the love in the boy, still sound asleep, curled warm and tight against the hollow of her body, his hands, smeared with grime, resting on his ribs. Easing away from him, she was able, for the first time, to imagine herself gone. And she knew how careless she'd been to allow him to come so close.

From *Women of Influence*, published by The Women's Press.

Harp Music

P A T R I C I A   G R A C E

THERE IS a girl. She was playing a harp. I forgot about her for fifty years but when I saw her again I remembered how I liked her. Loved her.

Because of my resolution to scale down, to stop being everything to everyone and to prioritise time, I wasn't enthusiastic about going to the school gala. I'd intended giving Jemma twenty bucks as my contribution so that I could stay home and get on with the work. I would have a warm room, my tapes and books, my neat notes and I would begin this weekend.

But the grandkids rang me about the gala. 'We're in the orchestra,' they said. 'And the kapa haka.'

'I'll bring your cousins,' I said. 'Lana, Tana and Banana,' (to crack them up). 'Aunty Jem's coming with Tiria. Your uncles'll come too I suppose, in time for lunch.'

'Neat,' and 'Choice,' they said from the phone and the extension.

In Room Four we sat on baby chairs with our knees in our chins. The little grandkids weren't overawed at all by the big children with their recorders, glokenspiels, tambourines, xylophones, bells, chimes, triangles, drums, shakers and clappers. While we waited I had this idea of changing all the first letters of instruments to bring about decorders, blokenspiels, pylophones, bambourines, pells, himes, hiangles, brums, takers and lappers. It pleased me for a time, then thought I'd better concentrate because the little grandkids were coming to a high pitch, taking no notice of the teacher bossing. They wanted to go outside, wanted their faces painted, wanted a pony ride, a hot dog. I was happy with their lack of silence.

'After, after.'

'Later, later.'

'Sit down.'

'Sit on a little chair.'

There is a girl. She was sitting on a little chair and could not speak because she had only wrong language to use. There was a voice. 'Stand up when I speak to you. Answer me, answer me at once,' it said.

Keri, who is wearing two dresses, and Rawiri, who has a T-shirt on over the top of a sweat shirt, are rolling their eyes at me trying not to show too much of their importance. It's not me that makes them weird. Pit-a-pat, pit-a-pat hear the sound of falling rain, pit-a-pat, pit-a-pat, on my window pane. Sometimes in strange surroundings you can forget who you are. Drink to me only with thine eyes, Hine e Hine, softlee, softlee, catchee monkee. Well, not so strange, just not an everyday environment these days. I feel fat and forgetful surrounded by miniatures.

As well as the real children there are cutouts of children standing by cutouts of houses, pasted against crayoned and painted roads, telegraph poles, trees, flowers and hills. Some of the cutout children are clothed in skirts and trousers of coloured cotton and corduroy, while others have clothes that have been painted or felt-tipped on. Some have wool hair. In the thick brushwork of sky there are two smiling suns, a crescent of moon, a stick of lightning and a fall of rain.

The opposite wall is top to toe in stories that begin with 'I am'. I am laughing. I am crying. I am jumping. I am Superman. I am at the grandmother's house. I am Michelangelo. I am at home. I am. I am going to McDonald's.

Me? I am forgetful among the cushions and story books, blocks and dress-ups, mini house with its furniture dishes pots and pans all in smallness. There are collections of leaves, twigs, stones, shells, buttons, containers, plastic spoons, icecream sticks, egg shells, cartons and cards. And then all the hangings – litter mobiles, story mobiles, light catchers, wind catchers and instructions in suspension. Benches, screens, dividers. You can forget, become part of a collage where you may see yourself stuck – button-eyed, stick-legged, hands like sated ticks. Hang if you don't remember.

There is a girl. She was picking at her muddy skin, picking, picking until the worms appeared. 'Fleas and maggots, fleas and maggots, mungie mungie typo,' the voices sang.

Coins of faces, the striker pausing, the taut space between the tick and the brum, the notes decording, the tapering pells and himes. I make a cup of my left hand and with the other, clap over this hollow that I have made. I'm proud of my echoey ovations and my eyeing grandchildren.

Last time I was in a school was when I went up to the college to try and persuade the timetabler to allow Pere to take the subjects he wanted. His groupings were wrong and timetabling wouldn't allow it, I was told.

'Is this school for kids or is it for timetables?' I asked, trying to be smart.

'He has to select from each group, take subjects that fit together – like Maths and Science,' the timetabler said.

'Is this school for kids or is it for subjects?' I asked, getting bumptious.

'Art, Mathematics, Agriculture and Maori don't go together,' he told me. 'They're in different groupings.' He wanted to give me a printout to prove what he had said was true, but I didn't want to look at any printout. I could feel myself losing ground and didn't need that shown to me in black and white.

'It's a weird combination, Art, Maths, Agriculture and Maori,' Mr Timetable said, smiling, walking me to the foyer trying to think of something joking and friendly to say to cheer me. 'What a weird son you've got. He'll have to make up his mind whether he wants to be an artist, an economist, a farmer or . . .' His smile left him and he blushed.

'A Maori,' I said. It shook him. I felt triumphant. I left.

The instruments are passed along to the ends of the rows where prefects disappear them into cupboards. Some kids leave and others come. Keri, who is smooth and beautiful and reminds me of midsummer plums, and Rawiri, who is thin and gawky with teeth and eyes that are too big for him, go to join a group out in the porch ready for the kapa haka items. Rawiri has his Michael doll tucked under one arm. Through the glass in the door I can see Rose Mei holding a guitar by its neck. She's shushing the kids and has a worried expression.

In they come singing, forming rows, synchronising. I feel guilty seeing the work that has gone into it. I could've come and helped Rose once a week if it wasn't for my resolution. She's worked on head and foot actions as well as arm and hand. Eyes too. The kids are good – know how to make it all happen between them and us. Good voices. The baby kids on their baby chairs are tranced.

'You missed it,' I said to two dreadlocked, bearded, sunglassed uncles, 'the orchestra and the kapa haka. You would've been proud of your nephew and niece.' They have with them Belle and Janes and enough tomato-sauced sausages on sticks for everyone.

'What did you think?' asked Michael doll.

'It was great. Tell Rawiri it was great,' I said to Michael doll.

'Did you hear that, Rawiri?'

'I heard.'

'Choice.'

'We want.'

'We want.'

'A pony ride.'

'Face paint.'

'Face paint.'

'Face.'

'Face.'

There is a girl. She was backed up against a garage wall spitting blood and stones.

'So tell me why you're wearing two dresses.'

'It's a dress and a skirt,' Keri says. 'A dress underneath and a skirt over top because I couldn't make up my mind.'

'Okay then, why a shirt over a jersey?'

'Because,' Michael doll replies, jigging into my face, 'if he puts the shirt on underneath the jersey no one will be able to read what it says — Save Our Planet.' How great my grandchildren are, how they save me. The realisation is debilitating. A pool of warm water I am.

'Here's fifteen bucks,' I say to Jemma. 'Get them all face paint, pony rides, whatever.'

'We don't need fifteen.'

'Take it, spend it on something. I don't want to take it home again.'

Soon we have a batman, a spiderwoman, a clown, two ninja turtles and another, I don't know what — a star maybe, going to queue up for ponies.

In the hall I am thin and alert. It's the kind of place where I often find myself in touch with me. But I don't find myself among the knitted dolls, embroidered bookmarks, lace covered tissue boxes, tulle bath cleaners, oven mitts and patchwork aprons. No.

I'm not there with potted apple mint, peppers, rosemary, garlic chives, lemon balm or parsley — nor with the cyclamen, fuchsia, rhipsalidopsis. African violets? I remember that they like warm water, steamy rooms, but I refuse to be interested in their juicy hands, their gentian faces and it's no use them looking at me winking little yellow eyes. Look here, Violet, you'd be sorry if I did. I'd neglect you, forget to water and steam bath you. You'd die.

I leave quickly. There are five dollars I have to spend on something but not on bonnets, bootees, matinee jackets, bibs, feeders, leggings, stretch-n-grows. Save me from all this.

Not dried flowers either, or straw ladies, pot pourri, lavender bags, perfumed sachets, pine cone owls, shell mice and turtles, driftwood families. Bark arrangements – which could be what they're meant to be, or could be Bach pieces, or a group of singing dogs. I'm pleased with myself about all that.

Most of the produce has gone. I could've, if there was a large banana cake, taken it home, chopped it up into square hunks and we'd have gobbled into it. But there's only one small cake left, lemon, with yellow sprinkles on white icing under a slime of gladwrap. There are a few bits of ginger crunch, a jar of marmalade, a bottle of pickle and an old cabbage. Hump.

But also there are a few baskets of sweets – fudge, coconut ice and burnt toffee. The baskets have been made from cut-in-half packets, cornflour and lasagne boxes that have been covered with fringes of crêpe paper. I could get one each for the ninjas, etc. But the parents won't like it because sweets'll make the kids hyper. They're already hyper so what's the difference?

But I resist. Anyway, the baskets are inferior. With a little more knowledge the basketmakers could've made vertical snips in the strips of crêpe, at five centimetre intervals, and using a knitting needle could've rolled and crimped the cut edges into petal shapes before layering them around the little boxes. For extra class and variegation they could've put two colours together before making the curls. I feel like telling someone this.

White elephant is more like it. Getting warm. What about a mouli, a jug element, toast racks, *Boy's Own Annual*, peeing boy decanter, firescreens, paua shell frogs, plaster girl with cat, handlebars, Platters records, pop beads, bar mirrors, rolls of wall-paper. Not really. Not even a Japanese fan? No, not really.

Missing from all this is Jemma and me's stall that we could've had, of weaving, to bring a different ethnicity to all this. Flax kono, we could've made and sold for three dollars each, and in them lemons, tomatoes and beans. Could've done three or four potato kits too which seem to be bigtime at the moment and were snatched in the first ten minutes at the Molesworth Street Market Day. Jemma could've done earrings, bracelets, headbands maybe. Even Keri, even Rawiri. I'm so glad to have succeeded in not having a stall, just as I'm pleased with myself not to have deprived Rose of slogging it out each week alone with the kapa haka group. I'm happy to have snubbed winking violet.

But pre-loved clothes? Oh. There's a knitted shawl of apple green that I can see could be made into a dress for a little girl, like Tiria, who at the moment is being a heavenly body on horseback. There are coats that could be made into shirts, skirts that could be trousers, jerseys that could be hats and gloves and slippers, or other jerseys. If I was a proper grandmother. But I'm thin and wide awake to myself now, determined not to buy up unwanted items that I will never remake into wanted.

Anyway there are perfect handknits that don't need remaking into anything. They are already it, yes. So I rummage through to find the right sizes, not that anyone seems to worry about sizes these days, except for big enough. Yes, yes. I stuff the woollies into a plastic bag that the keeper gives me, feeling excited and marvellous, and with only two dollars left to get rid of.

I queue up for tea and the fortune teller, telling the tea sellers that I don't drink tea but I'm keen on having the leaves read.

'We'll tip most of it out,' they say. 'Then you can just take a sip and blow on it a few times. That should do the trick.'

'You do believe, don't you,' the leaf reader said, 'that I'm going to tell you something important and of value to yourself?'

'Well I . . . um . . . had two dollars . . .'

'Tip it upside down on the saucer. Give it a turn or two.'

She is wearing two dresses too. The underneath one is floral crimplene with a scooped neckline. Over the top of it she has a gauzy green gown with a dippy hem which is caught across the middle of her by a large glass brooch. She has a round, kind face.

'You know,' she said, 'it's interesting isn't it, but someone like you just has to learn to use her time. So many commitments. It's always been a problem hasn't it? But let's not call it that, a problem. It's the difficulty of always being interested in everything, always wanting to know, have a hand in, have a say. And it's the competence that you get after a while. It's all right being good at things, being interested, getting involved, but then it traps you. You get pulled this way and that until it's too much. Too many demands. Well you'll have to leave some of it for others now. Delegate, you know.'

Who is this gauzy woman?

'Otherwise how will you ever be able to get on with this new undertaking. You need the time for yourself. It's difficult, isn't it, when you're not used to it, to take time?

'And there's a show, or something like that, that you'll attend. It'll have meaning for you, something misty.'

Who can this be?
So gauze and green,
With glass
Centring eye.

'Now what about the past?'

What indeed? Her old, kind face is blotchy – red, white and purple. It is an attractive face with old teeth that jut forward. Her eyes bulge in the way that buck-toothed people's eyes often do. Her fingers caress the cup as she turns it onto my past.

'Harp music. There's something here about harp music. Is that something you enjoy, harp music?'

'No, not harp in particular. I don't think. No I've never . . .'

'That's strange, because there's something here to do with . . . harp music. Definitely. So let's think about that. Perhaps it might be that something to do with harp music will bring forward a memory. It could be that that memory will hold something of significance for you, you know, help you to know or understand something. About yourself, to do with you. Because it's difficult to remember sometimes, you get involved, distracted, keep moving out to the edges, forget the core and lose the way back. Yes I think so. About you. Anyway think about that, about the harp music and it'll give you a boost, you'll see.'

All right I will, beautiful woman.

'Well that's it and it's been interesting I must say. It's been good, hasn't it, for you. Something about now, advice for you about all your involvements and giving some of it away, but you're already trying to, aren't you? All you need is the encouragement. Then something that you'll do in the future, the near future I'd say, attend a show of some sort. And something from the past which might be the most important of all, bringing a memory you know, to do with harp music.'

The ninjas are arguing about which one of them is Michelangelo. All of them, ninjas, spiderpeople, cats, batmen and heavenly bodies, are wearing odd socks because they're weird. Parents too.

'If you all line up,' I say, 'and look down, you'll see the mates of socks on each other, then you could all swap and have proper pairs.'

No one says anything. I can tell they're wondering why I would think they would ever want to do such a thing.

The Michelangelos are still at it. 'I always wanted to be Tom Mix,' I say. 'We had beachwood guns and we shanks's ponied along the sand being cowboys.'

They are underawed, even Keri, though she smiles and nods to humour me.

'Why don't you both be Michelangelo then?'

'I don't want to now, I want to be Raphael.'

'No I'm Raphael.'

'Is that all you bought?' I am asked in genuine surprise.

'How come you haven't bought a whole stall?'

'Whole hall?'

'Whole school?'

'It's not all. I got some stuff from the tealeaf woman for two dollars.'

'Well how come?' asked Jemma after I'd told.

'Don't know. She saw it in the tealeaves.'

'That's weird. I mean how did she know about the research and stuff?'

'Undertaking, she called it.'

'Sounds like shoplifted gruts.'

'And then when she said that about the misty show I thought of the exhibition that's coming up – that brochure . . .'

'That painting on the front of it. All the tipuna with their sombre eyeballs looking out through mists of skies and mists of scapes.'

'Scapes' is weird.

Kids are all upside down on the playground bars and so are their father-uncles, coins dropping out of their pockets. They're singing sad songs.

Does that make us all crazy? Is it me that makes them weird? Is the whole world wairangi, haurangi, porangi? Well hell! We've turned all these things against ourselves, haven't we? Look at the state of water now. Think what the wind is likely to bring to our lungs these days. Think of the big cloud coming – long, cold darknesses and having to live forever underground.

What? Going on a downer? But I reach.

'Thank goodness for woollies,' I say. I pull them all out as we make our way to the cars. There's a stripy jumper, an off-white cable knit jacket, a brown cardigan with duffle buttons, a grey jersey with soldiers back and front, a shell-stitched matinee jacket, a multi-coloured poncho, a blue hat with pompoms and a red hat with green ear flaps.

'Hup, two, three, four,' says the soldier batman kid, marching in the new old jersey. And hup, two, three, four the others repeat, marching along behind.

I decided to put some thought to harp music, but realise I need to get home to do the thinking, it's no use trying in amongst the hup, two, threes. I'll have to get rid of everyone, or if they come home with me I'll have to go to bed and let them get on with cooking stuff.

But when we get to the cars they all slam and toot away in different directions, all the ninjas, soldiers etc, swapped or given back to their part owners and shareholders.

So then I am alone and offended, facing an empty house. If I had banana cake they'd have come.

Anyway harp music. I needed to think about just that, if only to keep winters off me.

For a long time I walk about the darkening house touching

the walls, the furniture, the switches, sometimes switching them – on off, on off, on off. Round inside me. Eyes closed, knowing that I know every corner of this house.

Or do I?

Keeping in touch, and knowing that I won't do anything else until I know what it is

to do

with harp music.

And then she comes, the girl, from somewhere. From my hip. She has short black plaits and is wearing a school tunic and a white long-sleeved blouse. She looks at me then moves away and I see her running down a hillside dodging the stumps and stones, horse dung and thistles, stopping by an old fence near to her house.

It's a wire fence, but not the usual paddock fence of post and batten with five strands of number eight. It does have cross strands, double the usual number, but it has vertical strands as well, making a high fence of wire rectangles. The wire is much finer than number eight and has become rusty and brittle. There are places where it has broken, and several places where it has been mended by twisting and tying the strands together.

The girl stops running when she comes to the fence and walks along beside it bending or reaching up, to turn the twists and ties. She is setting up the orchestra in which she will be one of the players, and turning the knobs of the giant radio over which the music will be heard.

When she is satisfied that all the preparations have been completed she sits in the long grass close to the fence, rests a cheek against it and puts one arm through. Then with both hands she begins to pluck and stroke the strings, and it happens as it has happened before, the music.

The music is all around walking, then running, swirling, climbing, and she is part of the playing. There is an eye of moon in the sky and a journey down to the sea walking on rocks in a dress that is yellow. One part of the music has the beat of the sea. There's smoke from a far chimney going to the eye in the sky.

And she is lifting too, lifting to the moon-eye and looking down over water and rocks and trees and paddocks, but at the same time she is playing the music. There are people with faces like wide bowls, looking up at her.

After a time she descends and the music is fading. Soon it has all gone but she knows it is her own.

She walks beside the fence again turning the switches of her radio, and when everything is done she comes, leggy and laughing and pleased with herself, running towards me.

From *The Sky People*, published by The Women's Press.

A Sudden Trip Home in the Spring

ALICE WALKER

For the Wellesley Class

1

SARAH WALKED slowly off the tennis court, fingering the back
of her head, feeling the sturdy dark hair that grew there. She was
popular. As she walked along the path toward Talfinger Hall her
friends fell into place around her. They formed a warm jostling
group of six. Sarah, because she was taller than the rest, saw the
messenger first.

'Miss Davis,' he said, standing still until the group came abreast
of him, 'I've got a telegram for ye.' Brian was Irish and always
quite respectful. He stood with his cap in his hand until Sarah
took the telegram. Then he gave a nod that included all the
young ladies before he turned away. He was young and good-
looking, though annoyingly servile, and Sarah's friends twittered.

'Well, open it!' someone cried, for Sarah stood staring at the
yellow envelope, turning it over and over in her hand.

'Look at her,' said one of the girls, 'isn't she beautiful! Such
eyes, and hair, and *skin*!'

Sarah's tall, caplike hair framed a face of soft brown angles,
high cheekbones and large dark eyes. Her eyes enchanted her
friends because they always seemed to know more, and to find
more of life amusing, or sad, than Sarah cared to tell.

Her friends often teased Sarah about her beauty; they loved
dragging her out of her room so that their boyfriends, naive and
worldly young men from Princeton and Yale, could see her. They

never guessed she found this distasteful. She was gentle with her friends, and her outrage at their tactlessness did not show. She was most often inclined to pity them, though embarrassment sometimes drove her to fraudulent expressions. Now she smiled and raised eyes and arms to heaven. She acknowledged their unearned curiosity as a mother endures the prying impatience of a child. Her friends beamed love and envy upon her as she tore open the telegram.

'He's dead,' she said.

Her friends reached out for the telegram, their eyes on Sarah.

'It's her father,' one of them said softly. 'He died yesterday. Oh, Sarah,' the girl whimpered, 'I'm so sorry!'

'Me too.' 'So am I.' 'Is there anything we can do?'

But Sarah had walked away, head high and neck stiff.

'So graceful!' one of her friends said.

'Like a proud gazelle,' said another. Then they all trooped to their dormitories to change for supper.

Talfinger Hall was a pleasant dorm. The common room just off the entrance had been made into a small modern art gallery with some very good original paintings, lithographs and collages. Pieces were constantly being stolen.

Some of the girls could not resist an honest-to-God Chagall, signed (in the plate) by his own hand, though they could have afforded to purchase one from the gallery in town. Sarah Davis's room was next door to the gallery, but her walls were covered with inexpensive Gauguin reproductions, a Rubens ('The Head of a Negro'), a Modigliani and a Picasso. There was a full wall of her own drawings, all of black women. She found black men impossible to draw or to paint; she could not bear to trace defeat onto blank pages. Her women figures were matronly, massive of arm, with a weary victory showing in their eyes. Surrounded by Sarah's drawings was a red SNCC poster of a man holding a small girl whose face nestled in his shoulder. Sarah often felt she was the little girl whose face no one could see.

To leave Talfinger even for a few days filled Sarah with fear. Talfinger was her home now; it suited her better than any home she'd ever known. Perhaps she loved it because in winter there was a fragrant fireplace and snow outside her window. When hadn't she dreamed of fireplaces that really warmed, snow that almost pleasantly froze? Georgia seemed far away as she packed; she did not want to leave New York, where, her grandfather had liked to say, 'the devil hung out and caught young gals by the front of their dresses.' He had always believed the South the best place to live on earth (never mind that certain people invariably marred the landscape), and swore he expected to die no more than a few miles from where he had been born. There was tenacity even in the gray frame house he lived in, and in scrawny animals on his farm who regularly reproduced. He was the first person Sarah wanted to see when she got home.

There was a knock on the door of the adjoining bathroom, and Sarah's suite mate entered, a loud Bach concerto just finishing behind her. At first she stuck just her head into the room, but seeing Sarah fully dressed she trudged in and plopped down on the bed. She was a heavy blonde girl with large milk-white legs. Her eyes were small and her neck usually gray with grime.

'My, don't you look gorgeous,' she said.

'Ah, Pam,' said Sarah, waving her hand in disgust. In Georgia she knew that even to Pam she would be just another ordinarily attractive *colored* girl. In Georgia there were a million girls better looking. Pam wouldn't know that, of course; she'd never been to Georgia; she'd never even seen a black person to speak to, that is, before she met Sarah. One of her first poetic observations about Sarah was that she was 'a poppy in a field of winter roses.' She had found it weird that Sarah did not own more than one coat.

'Say listen, Sarah,' said Pam, 'I heard about your father. I'm sorry. I really am.'

'Thanks,' said Sarah.

'Is there anything we can do? I thought, well, maybe you'd want my father to get somebody to fly you down. He'd go himself but he's taking Mother to Madeira this week. You wouldn't have to worry about trains and things.'

Pamela's father was one of the richest men in the world, though no one ever mentioned it. Pam only alluded to it at times of crisis, when a friend might benefit from the use of a private plane, train, or ship; or, if someone wanted to study the characteristics of a totally secluded village, island or mountain, she might offer one of theirs. Sarah could not comprehend such wealth, and was always annoyed because Pam didn't look more like a billionaire's daughter. A billionaire's daughter, Sarah thought, should really be less horsey and brush her teeth more often.

'Gonna tell me what you're brooding about?' asked Pam.

Sarah stood in front of the radiator, her fingers resting on the window seat. Down below girls were coming up the hill from supper.

'I'm thinking,' she said, 'of the child's duty to his parents after they are dead.'

'Is that all?'

'Do you know,' asked Sarah, 'about Richard Wright and his father?'

Pamela frowned. Sarah looked down at her.

'Oh, I forgot,' she said with a sigh, 'they don't teach Wright here. The poshest school in the US, and the girls come out ignorant.' She looked at her watch, saw she had twenty minutes before her train. 'Really,' she said almost inaudibly, 'why Tears Eliot, Ezratic Pound, and even Sara Teacake, and no Wright?' She and Pamela thought ee cummings very clever with his perceptive spelling of great literary names.

'Is he a poet then?' asked Pam. She adored poetry, all poetry. Half of America's poetry she had, of course, not read, for the simple reason that she had never heard of it.

'No,' said Sarah, 'he wasn't a poet.' She felt weary. 'He was a man who wrote, a man who had trouble with his father.' She began to walk about the room, and came to stand below the picture of the old man and the little girl.

'When he was a child,' she continued, 'his father ran off with another woman, and one day when Richard and his mother went to ask him for money to buy food he laughingly rejected them. Richard, being very young, thought his father Godlike. Big, omnipotent, unpredictable, undependable and cruel. Entirely in control of his universe. Just like a god. But, many years later, after Wright had become a famous writer, he went down to Mississippi to visit his father. He found, instead of God, just an old watery-eyed field hand, bent from plowing, his teeth gone, smelling of manure. Richard realized that the most daring thing his "God" had done was run off with that other woman.'

'So?' asked Pam. 'What "duty" did he feel he owed the old man?'

'So,' said Sarah, 'that's what Wright wondered as he peered into that old shifty-eyed Mississippi Negro face. What was the duty of the son of a destroyed man? The son of a man whose vision had stopped at the edge of fields that weren't even his. Who was Wright without his father? Was he Wright the great writer? Wright the Communist? Wright the French farmer? Wright whose white wife could never accompany him to Mississippi? Was he, in fact, still his father's son? Or was he freed by his father's desertion to be nobody's son, to be his own father? Could he disavow his father and live? And if so, live as what? As whom? And for what purpose?'

'Well,' said Pam, swinging her hair over her shoulders and squinting her small eyes, 'if his father rejected him I don't see why Wright even bothered to go see him again. From what you've said, Wright earned the freedom to be whoever he wanted to be. To a strong man a father is not essential.'

'Maybe not,' said Sarah, 'but Wright's father was one faulty door in a house of many ancient rooms. Was that one faulty door to shut him off forever from the rest of the house? That was the question. And though he answered this question eloquently in his work, where it really counted, one can only wonder if he was able to answer it satisfactorily – or at all – in his life.'

'You're thinking of his father more as a symbol of something, aren't you?' asked Pam.

'I suppose,' said Sarah, taking a last look around her room. 'I see him as a door that refused to open, a hand that was always closed. A fist.'

Pamela walked with her to one of the college limousines, and in a few minutes she was at the station. The train to the city was just arriving.

'Have a nice trip,' said the middle-aged driver courteously, as she took her suitcase from him. But for about the thousandth time since she'd seen him, he winked at her.

Once away from her friends she did not miss them. The school was all they had in common. How could they ever know her if they were not allowed to know Wright, she wondered. She was interesting, 'beautiful', only because they had no idea what made her, charming only because they had no idea from where she came. And where they came from, though she glimpsed it – in themselves and in F Scott Fitzgerald – she was never to enter. She hadn't the inclination or the proper ticket.

2

Her father's body was in Sarah's old room. The bed had been taken down to make room for the flowers and chairs and casket. Sarah looked for a long time into the face, as if to find some answer to her questions written there. It was the same face, a dark Shakespearean head framed by gray, woolly hair and split almost in half by a short, gray mustache. It was a completely silent face, a shut face. But her father's face also looked fat, stuffed, and ready to burst. He wore a navy-blue suit, white shirt and black tie. Sarah bent and loosened the tie. Tears started behind her shoulder blades but did not reach her eyes.

'There's a rat here under the casket,' she called to her brother, who apparently did not hear her, for he did not come in. She was alone with her father, as she had rarely been when he was alive. When he was alive she had avoided him.

'Where's that girl at?' her father would ask. 'Done closed herself up in her room again,' he would answer himself.

For Sarah's mother had died in her sleep one night. Just gone to bed tired and never got up. And Sarah had blamed her father.

Stare the rat down, thought Sarah, surely that will help. *Perhaps it doesn't matter whether I misunderstood or never understood.*

'We moved so much looking for crops, a place to *live*,' her father had moaned, accompanied by Sarah's stony silence. 'The moving killed her. And now we have a real house, with *four* rooms, and a mailbox on the *porch*, and it's too late. She gone. *She* ain't here to see it.' On very bad days her father would not eat at all. At night he did not sleep.

Whatever had made her think she knew what love was or was not?

Here she was, Sarah Davis, immersed in Camusian philosophy, versed in many languages, a poppy, of all things, among winter roses. But before she became a poppy she was a native Georgian sunflower, but still had not spoken the language they both knew. Not to him.

Stare the rat down, she thought, and did. The rascal dropped his bold eyes and slunk away. Sarah felt she had, at least, accomplished something.

Why did she have to see the picture of her mother, the one on the mantel among all the religious doodads, come to life? Her mother had stood stout against the years, clean gray braids shining across the top of her head, her eyes snapping, protective. Talking to her father.

'He called you out your name, we'll leave this place today. Not tomorrow. That be too late. Today!' Her mother was magnificent in her quick decisions.

'But what about your garden, the children, the change of schools?' Her father would be holding, most likely, the wide brim of his hat in nervously twisting fingers.

'He called you out your name, we go!'

And go they would. Who knew exactly where, before they moved? Another soundless place, walls falling down, roofing gone; another face to please without leaving too much of her father's pride at his feet. But to Sarah then, no matter with what alacrity her father moved, foot-dragging alone was visible.

The moving killed her, her father had said, *but the moving was also love.*

Did it matter now that often he had threatened their lives with the rage of his despair? That once he had spanked the crying baby violently, who later died of something else altogether . . . and that the next day they moved?

'No,' said Sarah aloud, 'I don't think it does.'

'Huh?' It was her brother, tall, wiry, black, deceptively calm. As a child he'd had an irrepressible temper. As a grown man he was tensely smooth, like a river that any day will overflow its bed.

He had chosen a dull gray casket. Sarah wished for red. Was it Dylan Thomas who had said something grand about the dead offering 'deep, dark defiance'? It didn't matter; there were more ways to offer defiance than with a red casket.

'I was just thinking,' said Sarah, 'that with us Mama and Daddy were saying NO with capital letters.'

'I don't follow you,' said her brother. He had always been the activist in the family. He simply directed his calm rage against any obstacle that might exist, and awaited the consequences with the same serenity he awaited his sister's answer. Not for him the philosophical confusions and poetic observations that hung his sister up.

'That's because you're a radical preacher,' said Sarah, smiling up at him. 'You deliver your messages in person with your own body.' It excited her that her brother had at last imbued their childhood Sunday sermons with the reality of fighting for change. And saddened her that no matter how she looked at it this seemed more important than Medieval Art, Course 201.

3

'Yes, Grandma,' Sarah replied. 'Cresselton is for girls only, and *no*, Grandma, I am not pregnant.'

Her grandmother stood clutching the broad wooden handle of her black bag, which she held, with elbows bent, in front of her stomach. Her eyes glinted through round wire-framed glasses. She spat into the grass outside the privy. She had insisted that Sarah accompany her to the toilet which the body was being taken into the church. She had leaned heavily on Sarah's arm, her own arm thin and the flesh like crepe.

'I guess they teach you how to really handle the world,' she said. 'And who knows, the Lord is everywhere. I would like a whole lot to see a Great-Grand. You don't specially have to be married, you know. That's why I felt free to ask.' She reached into her bag and took out a Three Sixes bottle, which she proceeded to drink from, taking deep swift swallows with her head thrown back.

'There are very few black boys near Cresselton,' Sarah explained, watching the corn liquor leave the bottle in spurts and bubbles. 'Besides, I'm really caught up now in my painting and sculpting . . .' Should she mention how much she admired Giacometti's work? No, she decided. Even if her grandmother had heard of him, and Sarah was positive she had not, she would surely think his statues much too thin. This made Sarah smile and remember how difficult it had been to convince her grandmother that even if Cresselton had not given her a scholarship she would have managed to go there anyway. Why? Because she wanted somebody to teach her to paint and to sculpt, and Cresselton had the best teachers. Her grandmother's notion of a successful granddaughter was a married one, pregnant the first year.

'Well,' said her grandmother, placing the bottle with dignity back into her purse and gazing pleadingly into Sarah's face, 'I sure would 'preshate a Great-Grand.' Seeing her granddaughter's smile, she heaved a great sigh, and, walking rather haughtily over the stones and grass, made her way to the church steps.

As they walked down the aisle, Sarah's eyes rested on the back of her grandfather's head. He was sitting on the front middle bench in front of the casket, his hair extravagantly long and white and softly kinked. When she sat down beside him, her grandmother sitting next to him on the other side, he turned toward her and gently took her hand in his. Sarah briefly leaned her cheek against his shoulder and felt like a child again.

4

They had come twenty miles from town, on a dirt road, and the hot spring sun had drawn a steady rich scent from the honeysuckle vines along the way. The church was a bare, weather-beaten ghost of a building with hollow windows and a sagging door. Arsonists had once burned it to the ground, lighting the dry wood of the walls with the flames from the crosses they carried. The tall spreading red oak tree under which Sarah had played as a child still dominated the churchyard, stretching its branches widely from the roof of the church to the other side of the road.

After a short and eminently dignified service, during which Sarah and her grandfather alone did not cry, her father's casket was slid into the waiting hearse and taken the short distance to the cemetery, an overgrown wilderness whose stark white stones appeared to be the small ruins of an ancient civilization. There Sarah watched her grandfather from the corner of her eye. He did not seem to bend under the grief of burying a son. His back was straight, his eyes dry and clear. He was simply and solemnly heroic; a man who kept with pride his family's trust and his own grief. *It is strange*, Sarah thought, *that I never thought to paint him like this, simply as he stands; without anonymous meaningless people hovering beyond his profile; his face turned proud and brownly against the light.* The defeat that had frightened her in the faces of black men was the defeat of black forever defined by white. But that defeat was nowhere on her grandfather's face. He stood like a rock, outwardly calm, the comfort and support of the Davis family. The family alone defined him, and he was not about to let them down.

'One day I will paint you, Grandpa,' she said, as they turned to go. 'Just as you stand here now, with just' – she moved closer and touched his face with her hand – 'just the right stubborn tenseness of your cheek. Just that look of Yes and No in your eyes.'

'You wouldn't want to paint an old man like me,' he said, looking deep into her eyes from wherever his mind had been. 'If you want to make me, make me up in stone.'

The completed grave was plump and red. The wreaths of flowers were arranged all on one side so that from the road there appeared to be only a large mass of flowers. But already the wind was tugging at the rose petals and the rain was making dabs of faded color all over the green foam frames. In a week the displaced honeysuckle vines, the wild roses, the grapevines, the grass, would be back. Nothing would seem to have changed.

5

'What do you mean, come *home*?' Her brother seemed genuinely amused. 'We're all proud of you. How many black girls are at that school? Just *you*? Well, just one more besides you, and she's from the North. That's really something!'

'I'm glad you're pleased,' said Sarah.

'Pleased! Why, it's what Mama would have wanted, a good education for little Sarah; and what Dad would have wanted too, if he could have wanted anything after Mama died. You were always smart. When you were two and I was five you showed me how to eat ice cream without getting it all over me. First, you said, nip off the bottom of the cone with your teeth, and suck the ice cream down. I never knew *how* you were supposed to eat the stuff once it began to melt.'

'I don't know,' she said, 'sometimes you can want something a whole lot, only to find out later that it wasn't what you *needed* at all.'

Sarah shook her head, a frown coming between her eyes. 'I sometimes spend *weeks*,' she said, 'trying to sketch or paint a face that is unlike every other face around me, except, vaguely, for one. Can I help but wonder if I'm in the right place?'

Her brother smiled. 'You mean to tell me you spend *weeks* trying to draw one face, and you still wonder whether you're in the right place? You must be kidding!' He chucked her under the chin and laughed out loud. 'You learn how to draw the face,' he said, 'then you learn how to paint me and how to make Grandpa up in stone. Then you can come home or go live in Paris, France. It'll be the same thing.'

It was the unpreacherlike gaiety of his affection that made her cry. She leaned peacefully into her brother's arms. She wondered if Richard Wright had had a brother.

'You are my door to all the rooms,' she said. 'Don't ever close.'

And he said, 'I won't,' as if he understood what she meant.

6

'When will we see you again, young woman?' he asked later, as he drove her to the bus stop.

'I'll sneak up one day and surprise you,' she said.

At the bus stop, in front of a tiny service station, Sarah hugged her brother with all her strength. The white station attendant stopped his work to leer at them, his eyes bold and careless.

'Did you ever think,' said Sarah, 'that we are a very old people in a very young place?'

She watched her brother from a window of the bus; her eyes did not leave his face until the little station was out of sight and the big Greyhound lurched on its way toward Atlanta. She would fly from there to New York.

7

She took the train to the campus.

'My,' said one of her friends, 'you look wonderful! Home sure must agree with you!'

'Sarah was home?' Someone who didn't know asked. 'Oh, *great*, how was it?'

'Well, how was it?' went an echo in Sarah's head. The noise of the echo almost made her dizzy.

'How was it?' she asked aloud, searching for, and regaining, her balance.

'How was it?' She watched her reflection in a pair of smiling hazel eyes.

'It was fine,' she said slowly, returning the smile, thinking of her grandfather. 'Just fine.'

The girl's smile deepened. Sarah watched her swinging along toward the back tennis courts, hair blowing in the wind.

Stare the rat down, thought Sarah; *and whether it disappears or not, I am a woman in the world. I have buried my father, and shall soon know how to make my grandpa up in stone.*

From *You Can't Keep a Good Woman Down*, published by The Women's Press.

Lipstick, Stockings, Bras and Sex

....
CAROL MARA

MOIRA LOOKS in the mirror. She puts on the big brown overcoat. And the scarf. It is a winter's night. She pulls the scarf close across the top of her head, crosses the ends under her chin, then ties it around the back of her neck to enclose all her hair.

In the mirror a tight bound-up little face looks back. She leans closer to scratch at a pimple in the crease of her chin. Then lipstick, Soft Frosty Orange. Curex from Coles.

'Well, Moira,' she says to the face in the mirror, 'what would Margaret think of this?'

When they were in sixth class they used to sit, her and Margaret Andrews, under a fat palm tree at the edge of the playground. They had an old black Webster's dictionary laid out on the black asphalt, opened at a greasy page. They never read out loud. The only words to pass between them were: 'Here, read this one.' 'What does that mean?' 'Look up that other word.' 'This dictionary is hopeless.'

Snakes and ladders with too many snakes. Round and round they went, destined never to reach home, the snake always returning to eat its own tail.

'Ask your mother,' said Margaret.

'No,' was Moira's emphatic reply to the suggestion of forbidden fruit, knowledge that would surely corrupt her, 'you ask yours.'

'Maybe I will. In the holidays.'

'Will you tell me, if she tells you?' Moira asked.

'Maybe.'

Margaret was younger than Moira, too young for high school, but not too young to want the knowledge.

Moira, starting high school, had an extra day off after the holidays. She went back to the primary school to see Margaret on that day. They met at the fence. Moira climbed up and sat astride the wire horse. Margaret sat side-saddle. She looked at Moira's open legs then put her fingers to her mouth to emphasise a giggle. Moira knew what to ask.

'Did your mother tell you?'

'Yeah. Do you know?'

'Sort of,' Moira lied. 'Tell me what your mother said.'

Pop.

She waited while Margaret peeled the yellow gum from her top lip.

'It's easy,' Margaret said, as she rolled the gum back into a ball. 'The man puts his thing inside her hole.'

Moira knew about the man's thing.

'What hole? Not the one where the pee comes out?'

'No, you dope, another one, girls've got three.'

Margaret reached into her pocket and pulled out a black-and-silver lipstick case.

'Who gave you that?'

'My new dad,' she said.

'Did they get married then, real married?'

'Yep. It was beautiful, I was the bridesmaid.'

'You're not old enough to be a bridesmaid.'

'Yes I am, my dad said so.'

Margaret wound up the case to expose the rosy red lipstick.

'Here, put some on,' she offered.

Moira looked at the smooth red curve projecting from the case.

'No, my mother won't let me.'

Margaret stroked the lipstick across the back of her hand, then held it up to the other girl's face. 'Nice eh, real sexy too.'

'Is that all?' Moira said.

'What?'

'About, you know, sex.'

'Well, you have to move a bit and sometimes you get babies and sometimes you don't, just depends.'

'Oh. What on?'

'I don't know, how old you are I s'pose.'

'How old do you have to be?'

'Old enough to have babies I s'pose.'

'About this hole . . .'

The bell clanged on the other side of the building. The deputy stuck her head around the brick corner and gave a few extra rings in their direction.

'Gotta go,' said Margaret. 'Ask your own mum.'

Moira watched her go.

'Anyhow, I'll be twelve next week,' she called after Margaret.

Moira went to Sunday School. Her Aunty Em had given her three pairs of stockings, Coppertone, 15 denier. Her mother had put them in the bottom drawer, unopened, for when she was old enough. At Mrs Johnson's down the road she found some old garters.

The other girls wore stockings to Sunday School. When she left the house on Sundays Moira wore the garters under her skirt. At the corner she would duck into the phone booth and take off her socks. She could have put the socks in her purse, there was plenty of room, but instead she would tuck them under the garters tight around her thighs.

When she arrived at Sunday School the first time she did this, all the girls looked at her mockingly. One of them called out, 'Where's your socks dabba doo, baby blue?' They all joined in the chorus, 'Dabba doo, baby blue.'

She was glad then that the socks weren't in her purse. They would have seen them when she opened it for the collection. Tucking them under the garters made them her secret, her private knowledge.

Three pairs there were. In her bottom drawer. Her mother mightn't notice. She took them out one Saturday afternoon when her mother was out. She opened the packet; two shimmering legs slipped between her fingers. She eased them over her toes, her heels, careful not to catch the fine polished threads. Over the knees, up to her thighs. Then she rolled the garters over the two burnished legs. She lay on the bed and held her legs high, stretched them out long, bent her knees, pointed her toes and could hardly believe they were hers. She stroked the lustrous copper finish and turned her legs this way and that to catch the light from outside.

She would do it.

The next day she folded the stockings small and put them into her purse. At the phone booth she took off the socks as usual. This time she replaced them with the 15 denier Coppertone stockings, tucking the socks under the garters just the same.

They didn't notice at first. They were now focused on Johnny Parson's downy upper lip.

'They're nice,' one girl eventually said.

Another, 'So, baby blue's got stockings, all she needs now is a bra.'

How could they tell, she thought. Always something else to worry about.

Her mother noticed though.

'I see you've worn those stockings.'

'Yes,' she said.

And that was it.

One hot summer day her mother sent Moira to the fruit shop for a pound of beans. She liked the greengrocer. Italian he was. She liked the way he said 'Beansa beansa boppeda beansa'. She hoped he would say it that day and joke with her. Instead he was looking, just kept looking at her lemon nylon top. He wrapped the beans in newspaper and as he took her money he said, 'Grazie Miss'.

She felt strange and embarrassed as she left his shop. He'd never said that before. She looked down at the nylon top her mother had said would be cool on such a hot day. There she saw two plump pink buds pushing out against the thin nylon. For the rest of the way home she carried the parcel of beans up against her chest.

She began looking in the mirror to see how big they were getting and wondering when her mother would buy her a bra. There was a longing, even stronger than for the stockings, for that day to come.

She liked gym, she was good at it. The girls all had to change in the same room and leave their clothes on the benches. Two or three of the girls were 'well-developed'. They wore their bras proudly, made sure everyone saw them by pretending to modesty, wriggling into gym tunics under their blazers or hunching into corners and holding their arms across their chests. One day two other girls undressed to reveal new snowy white bras.

Edwina, whose uppermost place in the well-developed stakes had not been challenged, was incensed.

'Look at Terry James will ya, flat as a tack, who's she think she is? At least Jill's got something to put in it.'

Poor Terry.

Moira didn't yearn for a bra for a long time after that.

When Margaret arrived at the high school the next year, Moira had other friends.

The extra year at the top of the pile did a lot for Margaret. Her hair was teased, her face pancake tan and when she could get away with it, her eyes were outlined in ragged black.

But they had scripture lessons together. They sat up the back. Margaret sneered at the elderly woman who prayed for their souls; and wrote notes to Moira.

HAVE YOU HEARD OF ORAL?

YOU MEAN FRENCH ORAL?

NO STUPID! LOOK ON THE BACK WALL OF THE WEATHERSHED.

Moira did. It was horrible. She went back and back.

'Who draws them?' Moira asked.

'Beats me,' said Margaret.

Every week for about three months Margaret's notes directed her to a new spot: fourth toilet on the right; senior cloakroom back corner; lift up the seat on the first desk in Room 16.

In this way Moira learnt many things.

One day the note said:

MEET ME IN THE TOILETS AT RECESS.

She did, of course. Her curiosity was large.

Margaret guided her into the end toilet.

'I'll show you mine, if you show me yours.'

'What?' Moira felt a bit uneasy.

'Tits, what else?'

They undid their buttons and opened their blouses. Margaret undid her bra, Moira pulled up her singlet.

'Just babies,' Margaret said. 'Look at mine,' and she jumped up and down so that they bounced.

'Shh,' said Moira.

Margaret then took out a lipstick from her pocket.

'Look what I'm doing,' and she coloured in her nipples with the red lipstick.

'Let me do yours.'

'No.' Moira buttoned her blouse and left.

Next week the notes said:

I'M LEAVING THIS PRISON.

WHERE YOU GOING?

BOARDING SCHOOL IN THE COUNTRY.

WHY?

MY MUM SAYS SO AND THIS SCHOOLS STINKS.

After that, Moira searched all the regular places but never found another drawing.

Moira looks in the mirror.

'C'mon Moi, we'll be late,' her mother calls.

The lights in the church hall filter weak and yellow through dusty windows. Moira holds back. 'Focus on the Family: Mother and Daughter Night.' She thinks it is all so pointless. After Margaret. She keeps her head low as they enter. She wishes they'd come late and it was dark, the slides already started. She sees some little first-year girls looking at her closely and whispering behind their hands.

'That's Moira Burgess, she's a prefect, in fifth year!' she hears behind her back. She wants to leave, be out of there, not disgraced by her apparent lack of knowledge. She's glad when the slides start and the room darkens. She crosses her arms across her chest and can feel the rapid beat of her heart. Her armpits are warm and damp. The wool of her winter skirt is itchy against her thighs. Two shadowy women take it in turns to operate the projector or point a long stick at the neatly coloured-in diagrams of the male and female parts and speak coyly about how they should most properly join together. Moira wonders how it feels for real bodies and every so often reddens in the darkness at the stifled giggles in the row behind her.

A question and answer session follows, but it is left to the two smiling women to suggest the questions and then give their answers.

'Well, how was that?' her mother asks afterwards, when supper is about to be served.

'Fine,' she says. 'Now can we go?'

'Wouldn't you like a cup of tea?'

'No.'

On the way home Moira thinks about Margaret and wishes she knew where Margaret was and could write and tell her about that night. She knows exactly how she would end the letter:

PS THE DRAWINGS WERE HOPELESS.

From *Eva's Crossing*, published by Allen and Unwin.

Hand-me-downs

WAJIDA TABASSUM

'O H N O, Allah! I feel shy.'

'Why should you feel shy . . . haven't I taken off my clothes too . . .?'

'Hm . . .' Chamki shrank back a little further.

'Are you going to take them off or should I call Anna bi . . .' yelled Shehzadi Pasha whose veins coursed with the wish to command. Chamki used her small hands with some trepidation to take off her kurta first . . . then her pyjama . . . On Shehzadi Pasha's orders she jumped into the soapy tub with her.

When they had both bathed Shehzadi Pasha turned to Chamki. With condescending fondness which had in it a large measure of possessive arrogance, she asked, 'Now tell me, what clothes are you going to wear?'

'Clothes,' Chamki said with great seriousness. 'Just these . . . my blue kurta-pyjama.'

'These?!' Shehzadi Pasha shrieked and turned up her nose. 'These filthy, stinking ones? Then what's the use of having bathed in water . . .'

Chamki asked a question in reply, 'And what are you wearing, Pasha?'

'Me . . .,' Shehzadi Pasha said with easy pride, 'you know at the time of my bismillah my grandmother had an outfit with *chanak chanak* stitched for me . . . but why did you ask?'

Chamki was lost in thought, then she laughed, 'I was thinking . . .'

'What?' Shehzadi Pasha asked in some surprise. Just then they heard Anna bi shout, 'No, Pasha! You chased me out of the bathroom, now why are you chattering with this no-good fool? Hurry up, or else I'll tell Bi Pasha right now.'

Chamki spoke quickly, 'Pasha! I was thinking that if you and I exchange our clothes and become *odhni badal** sisters then I could also wear your clothes, no?'

'My clothes . . .? You mean all those clothes which are lying in my trunks?'

Chamki nodded uncertainly. Shehzadi Pasha was doubled up with laughter, 'Ao, what a foolish girl. You know you are a servant – you wear *my* discarded things. And all your life you'll wear my hand-me-downs.'

Then with infinite love which held more arrogance than any other feeling, Shehzadi Pasha tossed the dress that she had shed for the bath towards Chamki. 'Here, wear this. I have any number of other clothes.'

Chamki was incensed. 'Why should I? You wear *my* dress . . .' she said pointing to her soiled clothes.

Shehzadi Pasha hissed angrily, 'Anna bi, ANNA bi . . .'

Anna bi rattled the door which flew open since it wasn't really shut . . . 'Oh, so both the madams are still standing around naked . . .' She put her finger on her nose and spoke in mock anger.

Shehzadi Pasha immediately took down a soft pink towel and wrapped it around herself. Chamki stood as before. Anna bi glared at her daughter.

'And why did you take a dip in Pasha's bathtub . . .?'

'Shehzadi Pasha told me to bathe with her.' Anna bi looked around furtively to make sure nobody was around, then she hurriedly pulled her out of the tub and said, 'Get to the servant's rooms . . . quick . . . you might catch a chill . . . wear my clothes . . .' Chamki shrank back a little self-conciously. 'Don't wear these filthy clothes now. There is a kurta-pyjama in the red

---

* Friends so close that, like sisters, they can exchange and share each other's clothes.

box which Shehzadi Pasha gave you the other day . . . put that
on.'

As she stood there, the little seven-year-old thought deeply
and said haltingly, 'Ammavi, if Shehzadi Pasha and I are the
same age then why didn't she wear what I took off?'

'Just you wait, I'll go and tell Maina that Chamki said this to
me . . .'

Alarmed, Anna bi picked up Pasha and said soothingly, 'You
know, Pasha, this whore has gone crazy. Why should you tell
your Maina about her ranting? Don't play with her, don't even
speak to her. Just be silent and spit on her name, okay?'

Anna bi dressed Shehzadi Pasha up, combed and plaited her
hair, served her food, and when she was done with all her chores,
she reached her own room to find Chamki still standing
unclothed, as naked as the day she was born. Without missing a
heartbeat she began slapping her daughter. 'You'll pick up fights
with those who feed you, you forward old hag! Now if the bada
sarkar throws us out, where will we go, eh? Such a temper!'

According to Anna bi it was a matter of great good fortune
that she had been employed as a wet-nurse for Shehzadi Pasha.
Her diet was as rich and fastidiously chosen as any begum's
because, after all, she suckled the only daughter of the Nawab
Sahib. She got lots of clothes too, because it was imperative that
the wet-nurse stay absolutely clean. And the best part was that her
own daughter got any number of Shehzadi Pasha's hand-me-
downs. Getting clothes was usual, but quite often, silver orna-
ments and toys also came their way. And here was this girl: ever
since she had started growing old enough to understand anything
at all, her only fixation had been – why should I wear bi Pasha's
rejects? Sometimes she'd look at the mirror and wisely state,
'Ammavi, I'm much prettier than bi Pasha, aren't I? *You* make
her wear the clothes I discard.'

Anna bi would admonish her all the time. After all the privi-
ledged have a lot of power. If somebody got the slightest hint that
it was that damned Anna's daughter and not the real daughter of
the house who uttered such things, they'd surely cut off our hair

and noses and cast us out. As it is, the years of suckling were long past. It was the tradition among such households that the wet-nurse was sent away only on her death. Even so, you can expect to be pardoned only for those faults that are pardonable. Not for this!

Anna bi twisted Chamki's ear and said, 'I don't want to hear any more of this, I promise you. You are to wear bi Pasha's rejects all your life. Have you understood, you child of an ass?!'

The child of an ass stilled her tongue then but the lava continued to boil inside her.

When Shehzadi Pasha turned thirteen it was her first Namaz-e-Kaza. On the eighth day was her *gulpashi*. For this occasion her mother got her such a gorgeous, glittering dress that your eye could hardly stay fixed on it. It had pairs of golden bells sewed on so that whenever Pasha walked there was sound of many anklets-*chunn bunn*. In keeping with tradition even this exquisite, expensive *jora* was given away. Anna bi gleefully gathered up all these gifts and took them to her room. There she found Chamki, who by now was wiser and more self-respecting than her years would suggest. She said unhappily, 'Ammavi, it is one thing to take such gifts because we have little choice, but please don't feel so happy when you take them.'

'Just think, beta', Anna bi whispered, 'even if we were to sell this *jora* it would fetch not less than two hundred rupees. We're lucky to have found a place in such a house.'

With enormous longing Chamki said, 'Ammavi, I wish . . . my heart's desire is that I also give some of my old things to bi Pasha some time.'

Anna bi struck her forehead and wailed, 'Now look, you're getting older – learn what is good for you. What will I do if anybody hears you say such things? Have pity on my old bones at least.'

Seeing her mother weep, Chamki fell silent.

Maulvi Sahib started both bi Pasha and Chamki on their Quran Sharif lessons and the Urdu alphabet. Chamki showed much greater intelligence and interest than bi Pasha did. When both of them completed their first recital of the Quran, the senior Pasha got Chamki a new set of clothes of ordinary material, as a mark of favour. Though Chamki later got bi Pasha's heavy set, she treasured her own clothes more than her life. She felt no hint of slight in them. A pale orange dress was much better than numerous glittering clothes.

Now that Shehzadi Pasha was as educated as was desirable, and was the right age, appropriately enough there was talk of her marriage. The house became the hub for goldsmiths, tailors and traders. All Chamki could think of was that even on the day of the biggest celebration, the wedding, she would wear only those clothes which were her own, not somebody's rejects.

The senior Pasha was a woman of great virtue and compassion; she always considered the welfare of her servants as she did that of her own children. So she was just as concerned about Chamki's marriage as she was about Shehzadi Pasha's. Finally, after nagging Nawab Sahib, she found a suitable groom for Chamki, too. In the general hubbub of Shehzadi Pasha's wedding, Chamki's nikah could also be managed, she thought.

That day, a day before Shehzadi Pasha's nikah, the house was packed with guests. A large gaggle of girls made the whole place gay and noisy. Shehzadi Pasha sat among her friends with henna on her feet and said to Chamki, 'When you go to your husband's house, I'll put henna on yours.'

'Oh, God forbid!' said Anna bi fondly. 'May your enemies only have to touch her feet. That you said such a thing is good enough. Just pray that the boy she marries turns out to be as good and kind as yours.'

'But when is she getting married?' asked one of the young girls.

Shehzadi Pasha laughed the same arrogant laugh that she had as a child, 'There will be so many of my used things that her dowry is as good as ready.'

Rejects, discards, used goods . . . it was as if a thousand needles pierced Chamki's heart. She swallowed her tears and lay quietly in her room. As the sun went down the girls picked up the dholak again. Songs loaded with double entendre were sung. The previous night had been a *ratjaga* – an all-night celebration, and there was to be one tonight as well. In the courtyard at the back, the cooks were cooking various delicacies on a battery of fires. It seemed like broad daylight in the middle of the night, in the house.

Chamki's tearful beauty appeared even more attractive in her pale orange outfit. This was one dress which could lift her from the depths of her inferiority and reach her to the very skies. These were nobody's old clothes. This new dress, made of new material, had come her way but once in her life. The rest of it had been spent wearing Shehzadi Pasha's old things. And because her trousseau also consisted of Shehzadi Pasha's clothes she would have to use them for the rest of her life. *But bi Pasha, a daughter of Sayyads can be pushed only so far and no further – you'll see. You gave me one old thing after another. Now you see.*

She entered the house of the groom with a large plate of *malida*. The house was decorated with rows of lamps, and bustled with as much gaiety as the bride's. After all, the wedding was to take place the next morning.

In the huge house and general confusion nobody took any notice of Chamki. After enquiring here and there she reached the groom's chambers. Tired out after all the ceremonies of haldi and henna, the groom lay sprawled on his bed. As the curtain moved, he looked around and was transfixed.

A knee-length pale orange kurta, tight pyjamas stretched over rounded calves, a lightly embroidered, silver-dotted orange dupatta. Eyes which swam a little, soft, firm arms emerging from short sleeves, hair adorned with garlands of white flowers and a dangerously attractive smile playing on her lips! None of this was new, but a man who has spent the past several nights fantasising about a woman can be quite explosively susceptible, however respectable and well brought up he may be.

Night is an invitation to sin. Loneliness is what gives strength to transgression. Chamki looked at him in such a way that he felt his very bones turn brittle. She turned her face away with calculated swiftness. He stood up agitatedly and planted himself before her. Chamki sent him such a look from the corner of her eye that he felt he was going to pieces.

'Your name . . .?' he swallowed.

'Chamki,' and a lustrous smile lit up the moon-like loveliness of her face.

'How could you have had any other name . . .? You shine so . . . you could only be Chamki.' He put his hands on her shoulders with a tremor. His attitude was not that of the usual male who chats up girls to seduce them. His hands shook as he took hers and said, 'What do you have in this plate?'

Chamki replied encouragingly, 'I brought some *malida* for you. There was a *ratjaga* . . . at night.' She cut him to the quick as she smiled with inviting slowness, ' . . . to sweeten your tongue.'

'I don't want any *malida* to sweeten my tongue. I . . . we . . . yes . . .' and he brought his mouth close to hers for a taste of honey. Chamki gave herself up to his embrace. To rob him of his purity, to lose her own, to plunder all of them.

On the second day, the day of the bride's departure, Shehzadi Pasha went to give her bridal costume to her foster mother's daughter, according to the convention of the family. Chamki smiled and said, 'Pasha, all my life I lived with your used things, but now you, too . . .' She laughed like one possessed, ' . . . all your life something that I have used is for you . . .' Her manic laughter wouldn't stop.

Everyone thought the sorrow of parting from her childhood playmate had temporarily unhinged Chamki.

From *Truth Tales 2: The Slate of Life: Contemporary Writing by Indian Women*, published by The Women's Press.

Below Zero

ALISON WARD

H ELL FROZE over long ago.

When they asked me to make a documentary about a dinosaur in the Arctic, I agreed without even pretending I needed time to think it over. An unforgiving wasteland was exactly where I wanted to be.

I needed a break. I needed a break from making preachy little films for schools, about Man's Abuse of the Environment. I worried about poisoning the kids' minds with all that guilt and ugliness. I needed a break from lovers. I fell in love all the time and regretted it all the time. Let them touch your body, and they think it gives them the right to stick their fingers in your soul as well. As for the kind friends who pointed out that I shouldn't take life so seriously, I needed a break from them too.

I did the research: sat through the Polar Survival classes, and read the books of prehistoric fairy-tales about Laurasia and Gondwana, when all the world was a swampland mottled by spindly trees which bent, dripping, under a blazing white sky. The dinosaur came from those times. Its skeleton had been drifting northwards for millions of years, until the ice closed over it.

I took the same route as the dinosaur, only measured in hours of flying time rather than millions of years. It makes the imagination feverish, flying for droning hours with nothing to look at but sea and ice. I wondered about the dinosaur, vast indifferent creature without any other name. How would I feel standing inside a ribcage the size of a cathedral? And then I wondered about the leader of the excavation, Dr Thea Christiansen, who had devoted her last three summers to this skeleton in a wasteland. She was probably mad. I pictured her emerging from the Arctic mists, bundled up in caribou skins and flourishing an ice-axe. Moving or ridiculous? I didn't care. Either way, I was going to enjoy myself filming the story of a monster being hacked out of the ice by a crazy old paleontologist.

I was wrong. Thea wasn't old.

She shattered all my fantasies, right from the first time I saw her. She was dressed in sunglasses, bunny boots and a grubby parka lined with nylon fur. And she was sitting on a bright yellow skidoo, eating – this was what shocked me the most – eating an ice-cream. I was too stunned to say anything. Where were the caribou skins? the axe? the mania?

She smiled back at me, but when she took her sunglasses off her eyes were cool and hard, as though she guessed what I was thinking.

The next day, we quarrelled. I didn't want to waste my time doing here-we-are-in-the-Arctic scenes. I wanted to get straight to the dinosaur.

Thea refused to let me go near it.

I took a deep breath, put down my camera, and asked her why.

'You don't have enough experience.'

That was a ridiculous reason. I pointed out that I'd made three full-scale documentaries already. I wasn't exactly a novice. Hadn't she seen any of my work? The one about the woman with the hippopotamuses had won a prize, and –

She interrupted me. 'I know. I didn't mean that. Your work's very brilliant, very sharp. But it's too neat to be truthful.'

I let that one pass. It stung then and it still stings. I can't help how I am. I was born neat, one of those sweet, neat little girls who are supposed to grow up into sweet, neat little women. At any rate I grew up neat, with a knack for sidestepping all the messy things like having babies or asking questions without answers. What was wrong with that?

'Thea, if you're not going to let me film the dinosaur, why did you ask me to this death-by-freezing nowhere in the first place?'

She shrugged. 'I didn't ask. The Institute just told me you were coming, whether I wanted you or not.'

'Oh, really? The Institute was very grateful I accepted the job. No-one else would have. Who else would agree to spend all summer on ice, tell me that, for the sake of filming you and that skeleton out there – '

'I suppose you had your reasons.'

'Is there something wrong with the dinosaur, or what? Is it still alive? Is it dangerous?'

Her eyes widened, and then she laughed. I liked her when she laughed, even though I was angry with her.

'No,' she said, 'it's not alive.' She stood up and looked at me for a moment from the doorway. 'I'm sorry to disappoint you.'

This is all the film I managed to bring back: these reels here. It's surprising how much has survived, when you think about it, but I'm not sure how to make sense of what's left. They're not in any order except this: this was the last reel I took, and it's the last one I'll show you. Shall we look through the others now? Let's try this set: 'Research Station'.

Exteriors: very grand, sledgehammer photography. See this, all you tired viewers of other people's lives, lounging in front of your centrally-heated TV sets. A plateau of ice as wide as the sky and an ocean rolled out like sheet steel, splintered by icebergs two hundred feet tall. The research station, by the way, is the little string of blocks along the shoreline, underneath the cliff. I stood on the roof of the station powerhouse to get this next shot: the camera pointing up, sheer, to that great blister of sheeting and wooden props bursting out of the cliff face. Inside the blister, the dinosaur is still asleep. The excavation team won't start work until the weather's right, in about a month.

Interiors: Thea in her study, pondering over a huge claw. The camera moves close and stays a fraction too long over her hands: beautiful hands, broad and long-fingered, honey-coloured except for a few scars left by the frost. She's explaining how the bones are hewn out of the ice and numbered, one by one. It's her job to work out how they should all fit together, but – catch her smile, it's gone in a moment – that's not easy when nobody's seen a fossil skeleton quite like this before, and some of the pieces seem to be missing.

Me, at midnight. Alone. Wide awake. Hard to sleep when it's the sun that shines all night, not the moon. So I lie in my bunk for hours, counting sounds instead of sheep. Clatters, rustles, bangs and drips, all the machinery that keeps us alive.

I've stood in Thea's doorway, and watched her sleeping.

I go to the indicator and check the wind-speed. I hate that wind. It looks harmless enough, stirring the loose snow into grainy patterns along the ground; but step into it, and it hits you like a lash of broken glass.

There's no wind tonight. Tonight, I'm going to climb the forbidden cliff, and see the dinosaur for myself.

When you look down, the space between you and the ground seems to stretch. I'd often stood at the foot of the cliff, staring up fifty feet to the dinosaur and yes, it was high enough to make an exciting camera-angle but that was all. I'd never realised how terrifying fifty feet can be, when you're hanging on the highest rungs of a ladder.

I reached up and dragged myself onto the platform, trying to calm my mind by concentrating on the state of my body. My armpits were running like melted wax, and I couldn't stop my legs trembling.

Wise of me not to bring the camera, this first time. But I hadn't brought any lights either. I looked across at the bleary sun, praying for it to break out of the mist and not let me walk blind into the dinosaur's cavern.

Heavily, I turned back to the wall of sheeting over the entrance and snapped open the clasps, mumbling to myself.

'It's only a heap of old bones. Why be afraid?

There's enough light to see. . . .

See what? Is this what you came for?

Don't wait too long. Go in now. Go in.'

Colossal grey forms growing out of blue shadows. The ribs, arching up to the roof, further and higher than the light could reach, massive pillars of bone held in place by beams like flying buttresses. I stepped underneath them, holding my breath as though I were trespassing on their silence by being alive.

After a while, I began to see the outlines of bones breaking out of the ground, a blurred jumble of curves and dislocated slabs flung down at random. And then, as I reached out to feel them, the sunlight flared up. It streamed through the entrance, stabbing at the chips of ice on the rock face, and turning the whole vault of the cavern into a dark sky flickering with stars.

If I'd let myself, I might have stood gazing at these until the cold lulled me to sleep. I tore my eyes away and walked around to keep warm, exploring the rest of the skeleton. Snaking away behind the ribcage was a row of flanges, crushed into the rock and ending, a few feet up, in a skull.

I almost felt pity for it. Had its neck been broken by something in life, or only by the passing of the ages? Oh, this place was bad for me. I was getting lightheaded and sentimental. I turned back towards the entrance.

And I saw the crack for the first time.

It began in the middle of the ribcage and ran outwards as far as the platform, a slit only a few inches wide but too deep for the light to penetrate. I crouched down, reached inside it and then snatched my hand away. Had it been there when I came in? The skeleton had been opened up by a landslide. What if the cliff face had started to split away again, and the whole thing was going to collapse underneath me?

'You've seen it, then.'

Thea's voice cut across my panic like a slap. Sharp and cold. I got to my feet.

'I told you not to come here.' In the half-light, her eyes glittered like the ice-chips. 'It's dangerous, if you don't know what you're doing. Don't try to step over it. Go round.'

'Thea – '

'I said, go round. This way. Don't look like that.' She reached across the crack. 'Take my hand, if you're afraid of slipping.'

By the time we were back at the station, she seemed more thoughtful than angry. I told her I was sorry.

She shook her head. 'No, I should have warned you.'

'About the crack? Why didn't you?'

'I thought you might tell the Institute.'

She'd noticed the crack a few weeks before. It was growing wider. Sooner or later the face of the cliff would break up, and the remains of the dinosaur with it. If the Institute found out, they would close down the station. I sat stiffly, rubbing my head and listening to Thea slate the Institute as a bunch of termites who didn't understand anything.

'I don't think I understand either. What if somebody gets killed?'

'If I'm the only one up there, whether I get killed or not is up to me.'

'And the rest of the excavation team?'

'They're not due in for another month. Oh, then I'll have to say something about it. You're right. But not till then.'

I wasn't sure I believed her. But for the moment, I thought, why should I say anything about the crack either? I had a film to make. And Thea was part of that film, the part I cared most about. She went to sit with the dinosaur every day; she wanted its silent presence so much that she would rather risk her life than leave it. I asked her how long she thought the crack would hold.

'As long as it needs to.'

She sounded very sure, almost serene.

When I couldn't sleep, I tossed over other things now apart from the noises. The dinosaur, Thea, Thea, the dinosaur. I didn't understand either of them. Perhaps they were both mad. I fell asleep over an old photograph, this one here. Thea aged four, pushing a toy pram just like all the other little girls in the high street. But those aren't dolls nestling under the hood, they're dinosaurs. Mummy Stegosaurus and Baby Stegosaurus and old uncle Tyrannosaurus Rex.

'Didn't you have any dolls to play with, Thea?'

'A couple. I chopped them up and threw them to the dinosaurs for lunch.'

'Yes, I see . . . why do you think they fascinated you so much?'

'Is this one of your in-depth interviews? All right, let's have an in-depth interview. You've beat about the bush long enough. What do you really want to know?'

Point blank. 'What made you come here?'

'Boredom.'

I waited. If you wait long enough, most people will blurt out something else. Anything to fill up the gap. The battle of the silences. I lost.

'Try again, Thea. I want to hear about dark, irresistible forces. Tell me about your passion for dinosaurs.'

'Boredom is a dark, irresistible force.' She jerked her head forward and stared into my face. 'Do you believe in dinosaurs?'

'Doesn't everybody?'

'Two hundred years ago, nobody even dreamed of their existence. I was born believing in them. I wanted to see, I wanted to know, everything about them. How were they made? Why were they here? Where did they go when they died? I made up all kinds of answers, when I was small. And they were much better answers than the ones I read in books when I grew up.'

'What answers? You don't get those sort of answers out of books. Even I know that.'

'True, but where do you get them from? You'll laugh, I even tried sitting at the feet of all the great dinosaur experts. Anything to avoid thinking myself.'

'Did you get bored with all the answers, then?'

'No.' Then stretched out her legs, and yawned. 'I got bored with the questions. This blanket's a bit scratchy. I'll give you one of mine, you'll sleep better. Only the living can perceive the living, and all the dinosaurs are dead. It doesn't much matter what they were made of, and they didn't need any grand purpose for being here. Don't turn up the lighting like that. You'll make me look sick, like you did the last time.'

I nearly dropped the camera, trying to keep the focus as she rocked herself in and out of the light.

'Thea, there's a film in here. And it's running.'

'Am I boring it? Switch it off then. Let's go for a walk instead.'

The sun has shone all week. I meet Thea on her way back from an evening rendezvous with the dinosaur. She looks distracted. Has the crack widened again? Surely it has, with the heat . . .

'I pegged it over with extra sheeting.' She dismisses the problem. 'Do you want to see something beautiful? Bring your camera, if you like. It's not far.'

We walk along the shore, not too quickly, the sound of our boots in the shingle muffled by the vast curving silence all round.

'Can't you get used to living here? Is it too sad for you?'

Sad, that was a curious word for her to use. I'd never thought of the Arctic as sad, only dead. Bare and cold and white, world without end.

'Too many Arctic travellers are haunted by the phantom of their own death: if you don't worry about it, it won't haunt you.'

Thea raised her eyebrows. 'Who told you that?'

'I'm not sure . . . I think I read it somewhere in my Polar Survival classes.'

I wondered if the thought of her own death haunted Thea too, but that's not the sort of question you can ask when you're out for an evening stroll.

'Thea, do you know where your dinosaurs went when they died?'

She laughed. 'No. I don't think they went anywhere. They

just existed for their own sake. Like these. That's why they're beautiful.' She took my arm and drew me to the top of the slope. 'This is what I wanted to show you.'

Flowers.

Thousands on thousands of tiny flowers. All along the tundra the ice has thawed into glittering blue and turquoise strips of melt-water, ribbons round the clusters of pink, yellow, white. I must tread carefully, so as not to crush a single one. Even these sunflowers only reach as high as my ankles.

I might have spent hours filming them. Wide-angles, close-ups, more light, less light, faster and faster film as the sun sank. The last one I took was this little blue flower, standing apart from the rest. I knelt down beside it, in the snow.

In a few weeks they'll be gone. And me?

'You don't belong here,' Thea said.

'No, I don't belong here.' I stopped, feeling her eyes on me. I wanted to tell her that I didn't stay just because it was a job, to make a film. I didn't care about that anymore. I stayed now because this was where she was.

She pulled off her gloves and bent down to touch the flower. Its petals were closing up. Then she held my face in both her hands, and kissed my forehead.

Twilight, the spell of ambiguity. 'We should go back now.'

The sun was so low that our shadows reached almost to the far end of the shore.

She takes my lips, slowly, and her teeth are sharp. Even her sweat is cold, it smells of the snow. She drags her fingers down my back and I shiver. I want to cry out: Thea, you're freezing me! How many times have I felt warm, close to her? I'm afraid of her now. I touch her and all I can feel is the skeleton under the skin.

They didn't go anywhere when they died. They existed for their own sake, and that's what makes them beautiful.

I know now, this place is too sad and I don't belong here. Tomorrow, or the day after, or the day after that, I'll leave. I twist myself out of her arms.

'Come here.'

'Thea, I'm cold.'

'Come here.'

That's not blood I can feel shimmering through my veins, it's melt-water. It seeps out of me with despair, not longing. If I reach out and touch her again, I won't be able to tear my hands away. She knows that. I grip her shoulders and bite back, hating her, listening to her breath hissing in my ear. Is it my rage or hers, filling my whole body? I could weep with it. Thea, Thea, Thea, I don't want this, but it's too late. She's enjoying my rage, riding it as it moves and thickens and swells in waves, tensing, flexing her muscles to dance with mine. Oh, I want to slow the dancing. I want this wave to rise and rise upwards, and never break. But it roars away, finite, to the point where it hangs motionless, and then shudders, and bursts apart.

We lie silent for a time, listening to the whispers behind each other's eyes.

Then she's gone.

Everyone was very kind, very understanding when I came home and said I didn't want to go through with this film. The editing would have been too painful, I couldn't have been objective enough – well, you know all that, that's why you're here. It's up to you now to piece all these bits together into fifty minutes of prime time, with a break for the ice-cream ads. It's all right. I know your picture will be different from the one I would have made.

This is some footage of the gravestone. In Memoriam Thea Christiansen, who gave her life for science, time and place. You might want it. I didn't shoot it and I wouldn't have used it anyway. I like my truth neat, remember. Here's what I could have chosen: these few minutes I shot the day she showed me the flowers.

'Thea? Thea, look at me.'

She turns round slowly, smiling not quite into the camera, but somewhere beyond it. Then she tosses up a handful of ice-crystals, up into the sun, and the air between us sparkles as though it's caught fire.

Freeze it there, credits over, the end.

This last reel? Yes, I'll show it to you, but I won't let you use it. I'd sooner destroy it. I made it the night . . . that night she left me to shiver myself to sleep. I knew where she was going. Up to rest in peace with her dinosaur.

I followed her. I don't know why I took my camera, I still don't know. Perhaps I had some idea of taking her for the last time, because I was going to leave her.

She was sitting inside the vault of the ribcage, hugging her knees and staring out at the sky. She couldn't have known I was there behind her, at the back of the cavern, standing in the shadows underneath the skull. Then I heard the sound, once, twice, very softly. A sighing rumble that vibrated through the dinosaur's bones. But Thea only nodded and touched the bones as though to soothe them, and kept looking at the sky. I shifted the camera onto my shoulder and turned it towards her.

I can't sit still and watch what happened then. The thing that haunts me and terrifies me most about this piece of film is that it's soundless. No, let it run. Watch the sheeting alongside Thea's leg, the sheeting over the crack. It's stretching, tearing away from the pegs either side. Then the bone shift, leaning inwards over that great dark wound opening up the ground. Thea's running towards me, through the cracked arches of the ribs, scrambling for the bones still sunk into the rock at the back, like the skull I'm clinging to. Even if the edge of the cliff collapses, these bones might hold. And if I let go with one hand, I could reach down to her.

Only I don't let go. I leave her out of reach.

The platform heaves and vomits out slabs of rock, wood, steel, down onto the station below. The whole ribcage is tilting, dragging Thea over with it and crushing her legs. Her eyes are still open. Is she looking at me, that albatross of a camera still hanging round my neck, watching her slide away? I can't be sure. I don't think it hurts her anymore. She doesn't even seem to be afraid.

From *In and Out of Time: Lesbian Feminist Fiction*, published by Onlywomen Press.

The Loveliness of
the Long-Distance Runner

SARA MAITLAND

I SIT at my desk and make a list of all the things I am not going
to think about for the next four-and-a-half hours. Although it is
still early the day is conducive to laziness – hot and golden. I am
determined that I will not be lazy. The list reads:

1. My lover is running in an organised marathon race. I hate it.
2. Pheidippides, the Greek who ran the first Marathon, dropped
dead at the end of it. And his marathon was four miles shorter
than hers is going to be. There is also heat stroke, torn achilles
tendons, shin splints and cramp. Any and all of which, including
the first option, will serve her right. And will also break my
heart.
3. The women who are going to support her, love her, pour water
down her back and drinks down her throat are not me. I am
jealous of them.
4. Marathon running is a goddam competitive, sexist, lousy thing
to do.
5. My lover has the most beautiful body in the world. Because
she runs. I fell in love with her because she had the most beautiful
body I had ever seen. What, when it comes down to it, is the
difference between my devouring of her as a sex-object and her
competitive running? Anyway she says that she does not run
competitively. Anyway I say that I do not any longer love her
just because she has the most beautiful body.

Now she will be doing her warm-up exercises. I know these
well, as she does them every day. She was doing them the first
time I saw her. I had gone to the country to stay the weekend

105

with her sister, who's a lawyer colleague of mine and a good friend. We were doing some work together. We were sitting in her living room and she was feeding her baby and Jane came in, in running shorts, T-shirt and yards and yards of leg. Katy had often joked about her sister who was a games mistress in an all-girls' school, and I assumed that this was she. Standing by the front door, with the sun on her hair, she started these amazing exercises. She stretched herself from the waist and put her hands flat on the floor; she took her slender foot in her hand and bent over backwards. The blue shorts strained slightly; there was nothing spare on her, just miles and miles of tight, hard, thin muscle. And as she exhibited all this peerless flesh she chatted casually of this and that – how's the baby, and where she was going to run. She disappeared through the door. I said to Katy,

'Does she know I'm gay?'

Katy grinned and said, 'Oh, yes.'

'I feel set up.'

'That's what they're called – setting-up exercises.'

I felt very angry. Katy laughed and said, 'She is too.'

'Is what?' I asked.

'Gay.' I melted into a pool of desire.

It's better to have started. The pre-race excitement makes me feel a little sick. Tension. But also . . . people punching the air and shouting 'Let's go.' Psyching themselves up. Casing each other out. Who's better than who? Don't like it. Don't want to do it. Wish I hadn't worn this T-shirt. It has 'I am a feminist jogger' on it. Beth and Emma gave it to me. Turns people on though. Men. Not on to me but on to beating me. I won't care. There's a high on starting though, crossing the line. Good to be going, good to have got here. Doesn't feel different because someone has called it a marathon, rather than a good long run. Keep it that way. But I would like to break three-and-a-half hours. Step by step. Feel good. Fitter than I've ever been in my life, and I like it. Don't care what Sally says. Mad to despise body when she loves it so. Dualist. I like running. Like me running. Space and good feeling. Want to run clear of this crowd – too many people, too many paces. Want to find someone to run my own pace with. Have to wait. Pace; endurance; deferment of pleasure; patience; power. Sally ought to like it – likes the benefits alright. Bloke nearby wearing a T-shirt that reads, 'Runners make the best lovers'. He grins at me. Bastard. I'll show him: run for the Women's Movement. A trick. Keep the rules. My number one rule is 'run for yourself'. But I bet I can run faster than him.

Hurt myself running once, because of that. Ran a ten-mile race, years ago, with Annie, meant to be a fun-run and no sweat. There was this jock; a real pig; he kept passing us, dawdling, letting us pass him, passing again. And every time these remarks – the vaseline stains from our nipples, or women getting him too turned on to run. Stuff like that; and finally he runs off, all sprightly and tough, patronising. We ran on. Came into the last mile or so and there he was in front of us, tiring. I could see he was tired. 'Shall we?' I said to Annie, but she was tired too. 'Go on then,' she was laughing at me, and I did. Hitched up a gear or two, felt great, zoomed down the hill after him, cruised alongside, made it look easy, said, 'Hello, sweetheart, you looked tired' and sailed on. Grinned back over my shoulder, he had to know who it was, and pulled a muscle in my neck. Didn't care – he was really pissed off. Glided over the finishing line and felt great for twenty minutes. Then I felt bad; should have known better – my neck hurt like hell, my legs cramped from over-running. But it wasn't just physical. Felt bad mentally. Playing those games.

Not today. Just run and feel good. Run into your own body and feel it. Feel road meeting foot, one by one, a good feeling. Wish Sally knew why I do it. Pray she'll come and see me finish. She won't. Stubborn bitch. Won't think about that. Just check leg muscles and pace and watch your ankles. Run.

If she likes to run that much of course I don't mind. It's nice some evenings when she goes out, and comes back and lies in the bath. A good salty woman. A flavour that I like. But I can't accept this marathon business: who wants to run 26 miles and 385 yards, in a competitive race? Jane does. For the last three months at least our lives have been taken over by those 26 miles, what we eat, what we do, where we go, and I have learned to hate every one of them. I've tried, 'Why?' I've asked over and over again; but she just says things like, 'because it's there, the ultimate.' Or 'Just once Sally, I'll never do it again.' I *bet*, I think viciously. Sometimes she rationalises: women have to do it. Or, it's important to the women she teaches. Or, it has to be a race because nowhere else is set up for it: you need the other runners, the solidarity, the motivation. 'Call it sisterhood. You can't do it alone. You need . . .' And I interrupt and say, 'You need the competition; you need people to beat. Can't you see?' And she says, 'You're wrong. You're also talking about something you know nothing about. So shut up. You'll just have to believe me: you need the other runners and mostly they need you and want you to finish. And the crowd wants you to finish, they say. I want to experience that solidarity, of other people wanting you to do what you want to do.' Which is a slap in the face for me, because I don't want her to do what she wants to do.

And yet – I love the leanness of her, which is a gift to me from marathon training. I love what her body is and what it can do, and go on doing and not be tired by doing. She has the most beautiful legs, hard, stripped down, with no wastage and her Achilles' tendons are like flexible rock. Running does that for her. And then I think, damn, damn, damn. I will not love her for those reasons; but I will love her because she is tough and enduring and wryly ironic. Because she is clear about what she wants and prepared to go through great pain to get it; and because her mind is clear, careful and still open to complexity. She wants to stop being a Phys. Ed. teacher because now that women are getting as much money for athletic programmes the authorities suddenly demand that they should get into competition, winning trips. Whereas when she started it was fun for her and for women being together as women, doing the things they had been laughed at for, as children.

She says I'm a dualist and she laughs at me. She says I want to separate body and soul while she runs them together. When she runs she thinks: not ABC like I think with my tidy well-trained mind, but in flashes – she'll trot out with some problem and run 12 or 15 miles and come home with the kinks smoothed out. She says that after eight or ten miles she hits a euphoric high – grows free – like meditation or something, but better. She tells me that I get steamed up through a combination of tension and inactivity. She can run out that stress and be perfectly relaxed while perfectly active. She comes clean. Ten or twelve miles at about eight minutes per mile: about where she'll be getting to now.

I have spent another half hour thinking about the things I was not going to think about. Tension and inactivity. I cannot concentrate the mind.

When I bend my head forward and Emma squeezes the sponge onto my neck, I can feel each separate drop of water flow down my back or over my shoulders and down between my breasts. I listen to my heart beat and it seems strong and sturdy. As I turn Emma's wrist to see her watch her blue veins seem translucent and fine. Mine seem like strong wires conducting energy. I don't want to drink and have it lying there in my stomach, but I know I should. Obedient, giving over to Emma, I suck the bottle. Tell myself I owe it to her. Her parents did not want her to spend a hot Saturday afternoon nursing her games teacher. When I'm back in rhythm I feel the benefits of the drink. Emma's is a good kid. Her parents' unnamed suspicions are correct. I was in love with a games teacher once. She was a big strong woman, full of energy. I pretended to share what the others thought and mocked her. We called her Tarzan and how I loved her. In secret dreams I wanted to be with her. 'You Tarzan, me Jane,' I would mutter, contemplating her badly-shaved underarms, and would fly with her through green trees, swing on lianas of delight. She was my first love; she helped make me a strong woman. The beauty, the immensity of her. When we swam she would hover over the side of the pool and as I looked up through the broken, sparkly water there she would be hauling me through with her strength.

Like Sally hauls me through bad dreams, looming over me in the night as I breathe up through the broken darkness. She hauls me through muddle with her sparkly mind. Her mind floats, green with sequinned points of fire. Sally's mind. Lovely. My mind wears Nike running shoes with the neat white flash curling back on itself. It fits well and leaves room for my toes to flex. If I weren't a games teacher I could be a feminist chiropodist – or a midwife. Teach other women the contours of their own bodies – show them the new places where their bodies can take them. Sally doesn't want to be taken – only in the head. Sex of course is hardly in her head. In the heart? My heart beats nearly 20 pulses a minute slower than hers: we test them together lying in the darkness, together. 'You'll die, you shit,' I want to yell at her. 'You'll die and leave me. Your heart isn't strong enough.' I never say it. Nice if your hearts matched. The Zulu warrior women could run fifty miles a day and fight at the end of it. Fifty miles together, perfectly in step, so the veldt drummed with it. Did their hearts beat as one? My heart can beat with theirs, slow and strong and efficient – pumping energy.

Jane de Chantal, after whom I was named, must have been a jogger. She first saw the Sacred Heart – how else could she have known that slow, rich stroke which is at the heart of everything? Especially back then when the idea of heart meant only emotions. But she was right. The body, the heart at the heart of it all: no brain, no clitoris without that strong slow heart. Thesis: was a seventeenth-century nun the first jogger? Come on; this is rubbish. Think about footstrike and stride length. Not this garbage. Only one Swedish garbage-collector, in the whole history of Swedish municipal rubbish collection, has ever worked through to retirement age – what perseverance, endurance. What a man. Person. Say garbage person. Sally says so. Love her. Damn her. She is my princess. I'm the younger son (say person) in the fairy story. But running is my wise animal. If I'm nice to my running it will give me good advice on how to win the princess. Float with it. Love it. Love her. There has to be a clue.

Emma is here again. Car? Bicycle? She can't have run it. She and Beth come out and give me another drink, wipe my face.

Lovely hands. I come down and look around. After twenty miles they say there are two sorts of smiles among runners – the smiles of those who are suffering and the smiles of those who aren't. 'You're running too fast,' says Beth, 'You're too high. Pace yourself, you silly twit. You're going to hurt.' 'No,' I say, 'I'm feeling good.' But I know she's right. Discipline counts. Self-discipline, but Beth will help with that. 'We need you to finish,' says Emma. 'Of course she'll finish,' says Beth. I love them and I run away from them, my mouth feeling good with orange juice and soda water. Ought to have been Sally though. Source of sweetness. How could she do this to me? How could she leave me? Desert me in the desert. Make a desert. This is my quest – my princess should be here. Princess: she'd hate that. I hate that. Running is disgusting; makes you think those thoughts. I hurt. I hurt and I am tired. They have lots of advice for this point in a marathon. They say think of all the months that are wasted if you stop now. But not wasted because I enjoyed them. They say, whoever wanted it to be easy? I did. They say, think of that man who runs marathons with only one leg. And that's meant to be inspirational. He's mad. We're all mad. There's no reason but pride. Well, pride then. Pride and the thought of Sally suppressing her gloating if I go home and say it hurt too much. I need a good reason to run into and through this tiredness.

Something stabs my eyes with orange. Nothing really hurt before but now it hurts. Takes me all of three paces to locate the hurt: cramp in the upper thighs. Sally's fault; I think of her and tense up. Ridiculous. But I'll be damned if I quit now. Run into the pain; I know it will go away and I don't believe it. Keep breathing steadily. It hurts. I know it hurts, shut up, shut up, shut up. Who cares if it hurts? I do. Don't do this. Seek out a shirt in front of you and look at the number. Keep looking at the number. 297. Do some sums with that. Can't think of any. Not divisible by 2, or 3, or 5. Nor 7.9? 9 into 29 goes 3.3 and carry 2. 9 into 27. Always works. If you can divide by something the cramp goes away. Is that where women go in childbirth – into the place of charms? All gay women should run marathons – gives them solidarity with their *labouring sisters. I feel sick instead. I look ahead and there is nothing but the long hill. Heartbreaking. I cannot.*

Shirt 297 belongs to a woman, a little older than me perhaps. I run beside her, she is tired too. I feel better and we run together. We exchange a smile. Ignore the fact that catching up with her gives me a lift. We exchange another smile. She is slowing. She grins and deliberately reduces her pace so that I can go ahead without feeling bad. That's love. I love her. I want to turn round, jog back and say, 'I will leave my lover for you.' 'Dear Sally,' I will write, 'I am leaving you for a lady who' (and Sally's mental red pencil will correct to 'whom') 'I met during the marathon and unlike you she was nice and generous to me.' Alternative letter, 'Dear Sally, I have quit because long-distance running brings you up against difficulties and cramps and I cannot take the pain.' Perseverance, endurance, patience and accepting love are part of running a marathon. She won't see it. Damn her.

Must be getting near now because there's a crowd watching. They'll laugh at me. 'Use the crowd,' say those who've been here before. 'They want you to finish. Use that.' Lies. Sally doesn't want me to finish. What sort of princess doesn't want the quest finished? Wants things cool and easy? Well pardon me, your Royal Highness. Royal Highness: the marathon is 26 miles and 385 yards long because some princess wanted to see the start of the 1908 Olympic Marathon from Windsor Palace and the finish from her box in the White City Stadium. Two miles longer than before. Now standardized. By appointment. Damn the Royal Princess. Damn Sally.

Finally I accept that I'm not going to do any work today. It takes me several more minutes to accept what that means – that I'm involved in that bloody race. People tend, I notice, to equate accepting with liking – but it's not that simple. I don't like it. But, accepting, I get the car out and drive to the shops and buy the most expensive bath oil I can find. It's so expensive that the box is perfectly modest – no advertising, no half-naked women. I like half-naked women as a matter of fact, but there are such things as principles. Impulsively I also buy some matching lotion, thinking that I will rub it on her feet tonight. Jane's long slender feet are one part of her body that owe nothing to running. This fact alone is enough to turn me into a foot fetishist.

After I have bought the stuff and slavered a bit over the thought of rubbing it into her poor battered feet (I worked it out once. Each foot hits the ground about 800 times per mile. The force of the impact is three times her weight. 122 pounds times 800 times 26 miles. It does not bear thinking about). I realise the implications of rubbing sweet ointment into the tired feet of the beloved person. At first I am embarassed and then I think, well Mary Magdalen is one way through the sex-object, true love dichotomy. Endurance, perseverance, love. She must have thought the crucifixion a bit mad too. Having got this far in acceptance I think that I might as well go down to the finish and make her happy. We've come a long way together. So I get back into the car and do just that.

It is true, actually. In the last few miles the crowd holds you together. This is not the noble hero against the world. Did I want that? But this is better. A little kid ducked under the rope and gave me a half-eaten ice-lolly – raspberry flavour. Didn't want it. Couldn't refuse such an act of love. Took it. Felt fine. Smiled. She smiled back. It was a joy. Thank you sister. The people roar for you, hold you through the sweat and the tears. They have no faces. The finishing line just is. Is there. You are meant to raise your arms and shout, 'Rejoice, we conquer' as you cross it. Like Pheidippides did when he entered Athens and history. And death. But all I think is 'Christ, I've let my anti-gravity muscles get tight.' They hurt. Sally is here. I don't believe it. Beth drapes a towel over my shoulders without making me stop moving. Emma appears, squeaking, 'Three hours, 26 and a half. That's great. That's bloody great.' I don't care. Sally has cool soft arms. I look for them. They hold me. 'This is a sentimental ending', I try to say. I'm dry. Beth gives me a beer. I cannot pour it properly. It flows over my chin, soft and cold, blissfully cold. I manage a grin and it spreads all over me. I

feel great. I lean against Sally again. I say, 'Never, never again.'
She grins back and, not without irony, says, 'Rejoice, we conquer.'

From *Women Fly when Men Aren't Watching: Short Stories*, published by Virago.

The Quilt Maker

ANGELA CARTER

ONE THEORY is, we make our destinies like blind men chucking paint at a wall; we never understand nor even see the marks we leave behind us. But not too much of the grandly accidental abstract expressionist about my life, I trust; oh, no. I always try to live on the best possible terms with my unconscious and let my right hand know what my left is doing and, fresh every morning, scrutinise my dreams. Abandon, therefore, or rather, deconstruct the blind-action painter metaphor; take it apart, formalise it, put it back together again, strive for something a touch more hard-edged, intentional, altogether less arty, for I do believe we all have the right to choose.

In patchwork, a neglected household art neglected, obviously, because my sex excelled in it – well, there you are; that's the way it's been, isn't it? Not that I have anything against fine art, mind; nevertheless, it took a hundred years for fine artists to catch up with the kind of brilliant abstraction that any ordinary housewife used to be able to put together in only a year, five years, ten years, without making a song and dance about it.

However, in patchwork, an infinitely flexible yet harmonious overall design is kept in the head and worked out in whatever material happens to turn up in the ragbag: party frocks, sackcloth, pieces of wedding-dress, of shroud, of bandage, dress shirts etc. Things that have been worn out or torn, remnants, bits and pieces left over from making blouses. One may appliqué upon one's patchwork birds, fruit and flowers that have been clipped

115

out of glazed chintz left over from covering armchairs or making curtains, and do all manner of things with this and that.

The final design is indeed modified by the availability of materials; but not, necessarily, much.

For the paper patterns from which she snipped out regular rectangles and hexagons of cloth, the thrifty housewife often used up old love letters.

With all patchwork, you must start in the middle and work outward, even on the kind they call 'crazy patchwork', which is made by feather-stitching together arbitrary shapes scissored out at the maker's whim.

Patience is a great quality in the maker of patchwork.

The more I think about it, the more I like this metaphor. You can really make this image work for its living; it synthesises perfectly both the miscellany of experience and the use we make of it.

Born and bred as I was in the Protestant north working-class tradition, I am also pleased with the metaphor's overtones of thrift and hard work.

Patchwork. Good.

Somewhere along my thirtieth year to heaven – a decade ago now I was in the Greyhound Bus Station in Houston, Texas, with a man I was then married to. He gave me an American coin of small denomination (he used to carry about all our money for us because he did not trust me with it). Individual compartments in a large vending machine in this bus station contained various cellophane-wrapped sandwiches, biscuits and candy bars. There was a compartment with two peaches in it, rough-cheeked Dixie Reds that looked like Victorian pincushions. One peach was big. The other peach was small. I conscientiously selected the smaller peach.

'Why did you do that?' asked the man to whom I was married.

'Somebody else might want the big peach,' I said,

'What's that to you?' he said.

I date my moral deterioration from this point.

No; honestly. Don't you see, from this peach story, how I was brought up? It wasn't – truly it wasn't – that I didn't think I deserved the big peach. Far from it. What it was, was that all my basic training, all my internalised values, told me to leave the big peach there for somebody who wanted it more than I did.

Wanted it; desire, more imperious by far than need. I had the greatest respect for the desires of other people, although, at that time, my own desires remained a mystery to me. Age has not clarified them except on matters of the flesh, in which now I know very well what I want; and that's quite enough of that, thank you. If you're looking for true confessions of that type, take your business to another shop. Thank you.

The point of this story is, if the man who was then my husband hadn't told me I was a fool to take the little peach, then I would never have left him because, in truth, he was, in a manner of speaking, always the little peach to me.

Formerly, I had been a lavish peach thief, but I learned to take the small one because I had never been punished, as follows:

Canned fruit was a very big deal in my social class when I was a kid and during the Age of Austerity, food-rationing and so on. Sunday teatime; guests; a glass bowl of canned peach slices on the table. Everybody gossiping and milling about and, by the time my mother put the teapot on the table, I had surreptitiously contrived to put away a good third of those peaches, thieving them out of the glass bowl with my crooked forepaw the way a cat catches goldfish. I would have been shall we say, for the sake of symmetry – ten years old; and chubby.

My mother caught me licking my sticky fingers and laughed and said I'd already had my share and wouldn't get any more, but when she filled the dishes up, I got just as much as anybody else.

I hope you understand, therefore, how, by the time two more decades had rolled away, it was perfectly natural for me to take the little peach; had I not always been loved enough to feel I had some to spare? What a dangerous state of mind I was in, then!

As any fool could have told him, my ex-husband is much happier with his new wife; as for me, there then ensued ten years of grab, grab, grab, didn't there, to make up for lost time.

Until it is like crashing a soft barrier, this collision of my internal calendar, on which dates melt like fudge, with the tender inexorability of time of which I am not, quite, yet, the ruins (although my skin fits less well than it did, my gums recede apace, I crumple like chiffon in the thigh). Forty.

The significance, the real significance, of the age of forty is that you are, along the allotted span, nearer to death than to birth. Along the lifeline I am now past the halfway mark. But, indeed, are we not ever, in some sense, past that halfway mark, because we know when we were born but we do not know . . .

So, having knocked about the four corners of the world awhile, the ex-peach thief came back to London, to the familiar seclusion of privet hedges and soiled lace curtains in the windows of tall, narrow terraces. Those streets that always seem to be sleeping, the secrecy of perpetual Sunday afternoons; and in the long, brick-walled back gardens, where the little town foxes who subsist off mice and garbage bark at night, there will be the soft pounce, sometimes, of an owl. The city is a thin layer on top of a wilderness that pokes through the paving stones, here and there, in tufts of grass and ragwort. Wood doves with mucky pink bosoms croon in the old trees at the bottom of the garden; we double-bar the door against burglars, but that's nothing new.

Next-door's cherry is coming out again. It's April's quick-change act: one day, bare; the next dripping its curds of bloom.

One day, once, sometime after the incident with the little peach, when I had put two oceans and a continent between myself and my ex-husband, while I was earning a Sadie Thompsonesque living as a barmaid in the Orient, I found myself, on a free weekend, riding through a flowering grove on the other side of the world with a young man who said: 'Me Butterfly, you Pinkerton.' And, though I denied it hotly at the time, so it proved, except, when I went away, it was for good. I never returned with an American friend, grant me sufficient good taste.

A small, moist, green wind blew the petals of the scattering cherry blossom through the open windows of the stopping train. They brushed his forehead and caught on his eyelashes and shook off on to the slatted wooden seats; we might have been a wedding party, except that we were pelted, not with confetti, but with the imagery of the beauty, the fragility, the fleetingness of the human condition.

'The blossoms always fall,' he said.

'Next year, they'll come again,' I said comfortably; I was a stranger here, I was not attuned to the sensibility, I believed that life was for living not for regret.

'What's that to me?' he said.

You used to say you would never forget me. That made me feel like the cherry blossom, here today and gone tomorrow; it is not the kind of thing one says to a person with whom one proposes to spend the rest of one's life, after all. And, after all that, for three hundred and fifty-two in each leap year, I never think of you, sometimes. I cast the image into the past, like a fishing line, and up it comes with a gold mask on the hook, a mask with real tears at the ends of its eyes, but tears which are no longer anybody's tears.

Time has drifted over your face.

The cherry tree in next-door's garden is forty feet high, tall as the house, and it has survived many years of neglect. In fact, it has not one but two tricks up its arboreal sleeve; each trick involves three sets of transformations and these it performs regularly as clockwork each year, the first in early, the second in late spring. Thus:

one day, in April, sticks; the day after, flowers; the third day, leaves. Then —

through May and early June, the cherries form and ripen until, one fine day, they are rosy and the birds come, the tree turns into a busy tower of birds admired by a tranced circle of cats below. (We are a neighbourhood rich in cats.) The day after, the tree bears nothing but cherry pits picked perfectly clean by quick, clever beaks, a stone tree.

The cherry is the principal monument of Letty's wild garden. How wonderfully unattended her garden grows all the soft months of the year, from April through September! Dandelions come before the swallow does and languorously blow away in drifts of fuzzy seed. Then up sprouts a long bolster of creeping buttercups. After that, bindweed distributes its white cornets everywhere, it climbs over everything in Letty's garden, it swarms up the concrete post that sustains the clothesline on which the lady who lives in the flat above Letty hangs her underclothes out to dry, by means of a pulley from her upstairs kitchen window. She never goes in to the garden. She and Letty have not been on speaking terms for twenty years.

I don't know why Letty and the lady upstairs fell out twenty years ago when the latter was younger than I, but Letty already an old woman. Now Letty is almost blind and almost deaf but, all the same, enjoys, I think, the changing colours of this disorder, the kaleidoscope of the seasons variegating the garden that neither she nor her late brother have touched since the war, perhaps for some now forgotten reason, perhaps for no reason.

Letty lives in the basement with her cat.

Correction. Used to live.

Oh, the salty realism with which the Middle Ages put skeletons on gravestones, with the motto: 'As I am now, so ye will be!' The birds will come and peck us bare.

I heard a dreadful wailing coming through the wall in the middle of the night. It could have been either of them, Letty or the lady upstairs, pissed out of their minds, perhaps, letting it all hang out, shrieking and howling, alone, driven demented by the heavy anonymous London silence of the fox-haunted night. Put my ear nervously to the wall to seek the source of the sound. 'Help!' said Letty in the basement. The cow that lives upstairs later claimed she never heard a cheep, tucked up under the eaves in dreamland sleep while I leaned on the doorbell for twenty minutes, seeking to rouse her. Letty went on calling 'Help!' Then I telephoned the police, who came flashing lights, wailing sirens, and double-parked dramatically, leaping out of the car, leaving the doors swinging; emergency call.

But they were wonderful. Wonderful. (We're not black, any of us, of course.) First, they tried the basement door, but it was bolted on the inside as a precaution against burglars. Then they tried to force the front door, but it wouldn't budge, so they smashed the glass in the front door and unfastened the catch from the inside. But Letty for fear of burglars, had locked herself securely in her basement bedroom, and her voice floated up the stairs: 'Help!'

So they battered her bedroom door open too, splintering the jamb, making a terrible mess. The cow upstairs, mind, sleeping sweetly throughout, or so she later claimed. Letty had fallen out of bed, bringing the bedclothes with her, knotting herself up in blankets, in a grey sheet, an old patchwork bedcover lightly streaked at one edge with dried shit, and she hadn't been able to pick herself up again, had lain in a helpless tangle on the floor calling for help until the coppers came and scooped her up and tucked her in and made all cosy. She wasn't surprised to see the police; hadn't she been calling: 'Help'? Hadn't help come?

'How old are you love,' the coppers said. Deaf as she is, she heard the question, the geriatric's customary trigger. 'Eighty,' she said. Her age is the last thing left to be proud of. (See how, with age, one defines oneself by age, as one did in childhood.)

Think of a number. Ten. Double it. Twenty. Add ten again. Thirty. And again. Forty. Double that. Eighty. If you reverse this image, you obtain something like those Russian wooden dolls, in which big babushka contains a middling babushka who contains a small babushka who contains a tiny babushka and so on *ad infinitum*.

But I am further away from the child I was, the child who stole the peaches, than I am from Letty. For one thing, the peach thief was a plump brunette; I am a skinny redhead.

Henna. I have had red hair for twenty years. (When Letty had already passed through middle-age.) I first dyed my hair red when I was twenty. I freshly henna'd my hair yesterday.

Henna is a dried herb sold in the form of a scum-green-coloured powder. You pour this powder into a bowl and add boiling water; you mix the powder into a paste using, say, the handle of a wooden spoon. (It is best not to let henna touch metal, or so they say.) This henna paste is no longer greyish, but now a dark vivid green, as if the hot water had revived the real colour of the living leaf, and it smells deliciously of spinach. You also add the juice of a half a lemon; this is supposed to 'fix' the final colour. Then you rub this hot, stiff paste into the roots of your hair.

(However did they first think of it?)

You're supposed to wear rubber gloves for this part of the process, but I can never be bothered to do that, so, for the first few days after I have refreshed my henna, my fingertips are as if heavily nicotine-stained. Once the green mud has been thickly applied to the hair, you wrap it in an impermeable substance – a polythene bag, or kitchen foil and leave it to cook. For one hour: auburn highlights. For three hours: a sort of vague russet halo around the head. Six hours: red as fire.

Mind you, henna from different *pays d'origines* has different effects – Persian henna, Egyptian henna, Pakistani henna, all these produce different tones of red, from that brick red usually associated with the idea of henna to a dark, burning, courtesan plum or cockatoo scarlet. I am a connoisseur of henna, by now, 'an unpretentious henna from the southern slope', that kind of thing. I've been every redhead in the book. But people think I am naturally redheaded and even make certain tempestuous allowances for me, as they did for Rita Hayworth, who purchased red hair at the same mythopoeic counter where Marilyn Monroe acquired her fatal fairness. Perhaps I first started dyeing my hair in order to acquire the privileged irrationality of redheads. Some men say they adore redheads. These men usually have very interesting psycho-sexual problems and shouldn't be let out without their mothers.

When I combed Letty's hair next morning, to get her ready for the ambulance, I saw telltale scales of henna'd dandruff lying along her scalp, although her hair itself is now a vague salt and pepper colour and, I hazard, has not been washed since about the time I was making the peach decision in the Houston, Texas, bus station. At that time, I had appropriately fruity – tangerine-coloured – hair in, I recall, a crewcut as brutal as that of Joan of Arc at the stake such as we daren't risk now, oh, no. Now we need shadows, my vain face and I; I wear my hair down to my shoulders now. At the moment, henna produces a reddish-gold tinge on me. That is because I am going grey.

Because the effect of henna is also modified by the real colour of the hair beneath. This is what it does to white hair:

In Turkey, in a small country town with a line of poplar trees along the horizon and a dirt-floored square, chickens, motorbikes, apricot sellers, and donkeys, a woman was haggling for those sesame-seed-coated bracelets of bread you can wear on your arm. From the back, she was small and slender; she was wearing loose, dark-blue trousers in a peasant print and a scarf wound round her head, but from beneath this scarf there fell the most wonderful long, thick, Rapunzel-like plait of golden hair. Pure gold; gold as a wedding ring. This single plait fell almost to her feet and was as thick as my two arms held together. I waited impatiently to see the face of this fairy-tale creature.

Stringing her breads on her wrist, she turned; and she was old.

'What a life,' said Letty, as I combed her hair.

Of Letty's life I know nothing. I know one or two things about her: how long she has lived in this basement – since before I was born, how she used to live with an older brother, who looked after her, an *older* brother. That he, last November, fell off a bus, what they call a 'platform accident', fell off the platform of a moving bus when it slowed for the stop at the bottom of the road and, falling, irreparably cracked his head on a kerbstone.

Last November, just before the platform accident, her brother came knocking at our door to see if we could help him with a light that did not work. The light in their flat did not work because the cable had rotted away. The landlord promised to send an electrician but the electrician never came. Letty and her brother used to pay two pounds fifty pence a week rent. From the landlord's point of view, this was not an economic rent; it would not cover his expenses on the house, rates etc. From the point of view of Letty and her late brother, this was not an economic rent, either, because they could not afford it.

Correction: Letty and her brother could not afford it because he was too proud to allow the household to avail itself of the services of the caring professions, social workers and so on. After her brother died, the caring professions visited Letty *en masse* and now her financial position is easier, her rent is paid for her.

Correction: *was* paid for her.

We know her name is Letty because she was banging out blindly in the dark kitchen as we/he looked at the fuse box and her brother said fretfully: 'Letty, give over!'

What Letty once saw and heard before the fallible senses betrayed her into a world of halftones and muted sounds is unknown to me. What she touched, what moved her, are mysteries to me. She is Atlantis to me. How she earned her living, why she and her brother came here first, all the real bricks and mortar of her life have collapsed into a rubble of forgotten past.

I cannot guess what were or are her desires.

She was softly fretful herself, she said: 'They're not going to take me away, are they?' Well, they won't let her stay here on her own, will they, not now she has proved that she can't be trusted to lie still in her own bed without tumbling out arse over tip in a trap of blankets, incapable of righting herself. After I combed her hair, when I brought her some tea, she asked me to fetch her porcelain teeth from a saucer on the dressing table, so that she could eat the biscuit. 'Sorry about that,' she said. She asked me who the person standing beside me was; it was my own reflection in the dressing-table mirror, but, all the same, oh, yes, she was in perfectly sound mind, if you stretch the definition of 'sound' only a very little. One must make allowances. One will do so for oneself.

She needed to sit up to drink tea, I lifted her. She was so frail it was like picking up a wicker basket with nothing inside it; I braced myself for a burden and there was none, she was as light as if her bones were filled with air like the bones of birds. I felt she needed weights, to keep her from floating up to the ceiling following her airy voice. Faint odour of the lion house in the bedroom and it was freezing cold, although, outside, a good deal of April sunshine and the first white flakes of cherry blossom shaking loose from the tight buds.

Letty's cat came and sat on the end of the bed. 'Hello, pussy,' said Letty.

One of those ill-kempt balls of fluff old ladies keep, this cat looks as if he's unravelling, its black fur has rusted and faded at the same time, but some cats are naturals for the caring professions – they will give you mute company long after anyone else has stopped tolerating your babbling, they don't judge, don't give a damn if you wet the bed and, when the eyesight fades, freely offer themselves for the consolation of still sentient fingertips. He kneads the shit-stained quilt with his paws and purrs.

The cow upstairs came down at last and denied all knowledge of last night's rumpus; she claimed she had slept so soundly she didn't hear the doorbell or the forced entry. She must have passed out or something, or else wasn't there at all but out on the town with her man friend. Or, her man friend was here with her *all the time* and she didn't want anybody to know so kept her head down. We see her man friend once or twice a week as he arrives crabwise to her door with the furtiveness of the adulterer. The cow upstairs is fiftyish as well preserved as if she'd sprayed herself all over with the hair lacquer that keeps her bright brown curls in tight discipline.

No love lost between her and Letty. 'What a health hazard! What a fire hazard!' Letty, downstairs, dreamily hallucinating in the icy basement as the cow upstairs watches me sweep up the broken glass on the hall floor. 'She oughtn't to be left. She ought to be in a home.' The final clincher: 'For her *own good*.'

Letty dreamily apostrophised the cat; they don't let cats into any old people's homes that I know of.

Then the social worker came; and the doctor; and, out of nowhere, a great-niece, probably summoned by the social worker, a great-niece in her late twenties with a great-great-niece clutching a teddy bear. Letty is pleased to see the great-great-niece, and this child is the first crack that appears in the picture that I'd built up of Letty's secluded, lonely old age. We hadn't realised there were kin; indeed, the great-niece puts us in our place good and proper. 'It's up to family now,' she said, so we curtsy and retreat, and this great-niece is sharp as a tack, busy as a bee, proprietorial yet tender with the old lady. 'Letty, what have you got up to now?' Warding us outsiders off; perhaps she is ashamed of the shit-stained quilt, the plastic bucket of piss beside Letty's bed.

As they were packing Letty's things in an airline bag the great-niece brought, the landlord – by a curious stroke of fate – chose this very day to collect Letty's rent and perked up no end, stroking his well-shaven chin, to hear the cow upstairs go on and on about how Letty could no longer cope, how she endangered property and life on the premises by forcing men to come and break down doors.

What a life.

Then the ambulance came.

Letty is going to spend a few days in hospital.

This street is, as estate agents say, rapidly improving; the lace curtains are coming down, the round paper lampshades going up like white balloons in each front room. The landlord had promised the cow upstairs five thousand pounds in her hand to move out after Letty goes, so that he can renovate the house and sell it with vacant possession for a tremendous profit.

We live in hard-nosed times.

The still unravished bride, the cherry tree, takes flowering possession of the wild garden; the ex-peach thief contemplates the prospect of ripe fruit the birds will eat, not I. Curious euphemism 'to go', meaning death, to depart on a journey.

Somewhere along another year to heaven, I elicited the following laborious explanation of male sexual response, which is the other side of the moon, the absolute mystery, the one thing I can never know.

'You put it in, which isn't boring. Then you rock backwards and forwards. That can get quite boring. Then you come. That's not boring.'

For 'you', read 'him'.

'You come; or as we Japanese say, go.'

Just so. *'Ikimasu,'* to go. The Japanese orgasmic departure renders the English orgasmic arrival, as if the event were reflected in the mirror and the significance of it altogether different – whatever significance it may have, that is. Desire disappears in its fulfilment, which is cold comfort for hot blood and the reason why there is no such thing as a happy ending.

Besides all this, Japanese puts all its verbs at the ends of its sentences, which helps to confuse the foreigner all the more, so it seemed to me they themselves never quite knew what they were saying half the time.

'Everything here is arsy-varsy.'

'No. Where you are is arsy-varsy.'

And never the twain shall meet. He loved to be bored; don't think he was contemptuously dismissive of the element of boredom inherent in sexual activity. He adored and venerated boredom. He said that dogs, for example, were never bored, nor birds, so, obviously, the capacity that distinguished man from the other higher mammals, from the scaled and feathered things, was that of boredom. The more bored one was, the more one expressed one's humanity.

He liked redheads. 'Europeans are so colourful,' he said.

He was a tricky bugger, that one, a Big Peach, all right; face of Gérard Philipe, soul of Nechaev. I grabbed, grabbed and grabbed and, since I did not have much experience in grabbing, often bit off more than I could chew. Exemplary fate of the plump peach-thief; someone refuses to be assimilated. Once a year, when I look at Letty's cherry tree in flower, I put the image to work, I see the petals fall on a face that looked as if it had been hammered out of gold, like the mask of Agamemnon which Schliemann found at Troy.

The mask turns into a shining carp and flips off the hook at the end of the fishing line. The one that got away.

Let me not romanticise you too much. Because what would I do if you *did* resurrect yourself? Came knocking at my door in all your foul, cool, chic of designer jeans and leather blouson and your pocket stuffed with GNP, arriving somewhat late in the day to make an honest woman of me as you sometimes used to threaten that you might? 'When you're least expecting it . . .' God, I'm forty, now. Forty! I had you marked down for a Demon Lover; what if indeed you popped up out of the grave of the heart bright as a button with an American car purring outside waiting to whisk me away to where the lilies grow on the bottom of the sea? 'I am now married to a house carpenter,' as the girl in the song exclaimed hurriedly. But all the same, off she went with the lovely cloven-footed one. But I wouldn't. Not I.

And how very inappropriate too, the language of antique ballads in which to address one who knew best the international language of the jukebox. You'd have one of those Wurlitzer Cadillacs you liked, that you envied GIS for, all ready to humiliate me with; it would be bellowing out quadraphonic sound. The

Everly Brothers. Jerry Lee Lewis. Early Presley. ('When I grow up,' you reveried, 'I'm going to Memphis to marry Presley.') You were altogether too much, you pure child of the late twentieth century, you person from the other side of the moon or mirror, and your hypothetical arrival is a catastrophe too terrifying to contemplate, even in the most plangent state of regret for one's youth.

I lead a quiet life in South London. I grind my coffee beans and drink my early cup to a spot of early baroque on the radio. I am now married to a house carpenter. Like the culture that created me, I am receding into the past at a rate of knots. Soon I'll need a whole row of footnotes if anybody under thirty-five is going to comprehend the least thing I say.

And yet . . .

Going out into the back garden to pick rosemary to put inside a chicken, the daffodils in the uncut grass, enough blackbirds out to make a pie.

Letty's cat sits on Letty's windowsill. The blinds are drawn; the social worker drew them five days ago before she drove off in her little Fiat to the hospital, following Letty in the ambulance. I call to Letty's cat but he doesn't turn his head. His fluff has turned to spikes, he looks spiny as a horse-chestnut husk.

Letty is in hospital supping broth from a spouted cup and, for all my kind heart, of which I am so proud, my empathy and so on, I myself had not given Letty's companion another thought until today, going out to pick rosemary with which to stuff a roast for our greedy dinners.

I called him again. At the third call, he turned his head. His eyes looked as if milk had been poured into them. The garden wall too high to climb since now I am less limber than I was, I chucked half the contents of a guilty tin of cat food over. Come and get it.

Letty's cat never moved, only stared at me with its curtained eyes. And then all the fat, sleek cats from every garden up and down came jumping, leaping, creeping to the unexpected feast and gobbled all down, every crumb, quick as a wink. What a lesson for a giver of charity! At the conclusion of this heartless banquet at which I'd been the thoughtless host, the company of well-cared-for beasts stretched their swollen bellies in the sun and licked themselves, and then, at last, Letty's cat heaved up on its shaky legs and launched itself, plop on to the grass.

I thought, perhaps he got a belated whiff of cat food and came for his share, too late, all gone. The other cats ignored him. He staggered when he landed but soon righted himself. He took no interest at all in the stains of cat food, though. He managed a few doddering steps among the dandelions. Then I thought he might be going to chew on a few stems of medicinal grass; but he did not so much lower his head towards it as let his head drop, as if he had no strength left to lift it. His sides were caved-in under stiff, voluminous fur. He had not been taking care of himself. He peered vaguely around, swaying.

You could almost have believed, not that he was waiting for the person who always fed him to come and feed him again as usual, but that he was pining for Letty herself.

Then his hind legs began to shudder involuntarily. He so convulsed himself with shuddering that his hind legs jerked off the ground; he danced. He jerked and shuddered, shuddered and jerked, until at last he vomited up a small amount of white liquid. Then he pulled himself to his feet again and lurched back to the windowsill. With a gigantic effort, he dragged himself up.

Later on, somebody jumped over the wall, more sprightly than I and left a bowl of bread and milk. But the cat ignored that too. Next day, both were still there, untouched.

The day after that, only the bowl of sour sops, and cherry blossom petals drifting across the vacant windowsill.

Small sins of omission remind one of the greater sins of omission; at least sins of commission have the excuse of choice, of intention. However:

May. A blowy, bright-blue, bright-green morning; I go out on the front steps with a shifting plastic sack of garbage and what do I see but the social worker's red Fiat putter to a halt next door.

In the hospital they'd henna'd Letty. An octogenarian redhead, my big babushka who contains my forty, my thirty, my twenty, my ten years within her fragile basket of bones, she has returned, not in a humiliating ambulance, but on her own two feet that she sets down more firmly than she did. She has put on a little weight. She has a better colour, not only in her hair but in her cheeks.

The landlord, foiled.

Escorted by the social worker, the district nurse, the home help, the abrasive yet not ungentle niece, Letty is escorted down the unswept, grass-grown basement stairs into her own scarcely used front door that someone with a key has remembered to unbolt from inside for her return. Her new cockatoo crest — whoever henna'd her really understood henna — points this way and that way as she makes sure that nothing in the street has changed, even if she can see only large blocks of light and shadow, hear, not the shrieking blackbirds, but only the twitch of the voices in her ear that shout: 'Carefully does it, Letty.'

'I can manage,' she said tetchily.

The door the policemen battered in closes upon her and her chattering entourage.

The window of the front room of the cow upstairs slams down, bang.

And what am I to make of that? I'd set it up so carefully, an enigmatic structure about evanescence and ageing and the mists of time, shadows lengthening, cherry blossom, forgetting, neglect, regret . . . the sadness, the sadness of it all . . .

But. Letty. Letty came home.

In the corner shop, the cow upstairs, mad as fire: 'They should have certified her'; the five grand the landlord promised her so that he could sell the house with vacant possession has blown away on the May wind that disintegrated the dandelion clocks. In Letty's garden now is the time for fierce yellow buttercups; the cherry blossom is over, no regrets.

I hope she is too old and too far gone to miss the cat.

Fat chance.

I hope she never wonders if the nice warm couple next door thought of feeding him.

But she has come home to die at her own apparently ample leisure in the comfort and privacy of her basement; she has exercised, has she not, her right to choose, she has turned all this into crazy patchwork.

Somewhere along my thirtieth year, I left a husband in a bus station in Houston, Texas, a town to which I have never returned, over a quarrel about a peach which, at the time, seemed to sum up the whole question of the rights of individuals within relationships, and, indeed, perhaps it did.

As you can tell from the colourful scraps of oriental brocade and Turkish homespun I have sewn into this bedcover, I then (call me Ishmael) wandered about for a while and sowed (or sewed) a wild oat or two into this useful domestic article, this product of thrift and imagination, with which I hope to cover myself in my old age to keep my brittle bones warm. (How cold it is in Letty's basement.)

But, okay, so I always said the blossom would come back again, but Letty's return from the clean white grave of the geriatric ward is *ridiculous!* And, furthermore, when I went out into the garden to pick a few tulips, there he is, on the other side of the brick wall lolling voluptuously among the creeping buttercups, fat as butter himself – Letty's been feeding him up.

'I'm pleased to see *you*,' I said.

In a Japanese folk tale it would be the ghost of her cat, rusty and tactile as in life, the poor cat pining itself from death to life again to come to the back door at the sound of her voice. But we are in South London on a spring morning. Lorries fart and splutter along the Wandsworth Road. Capital Radio is braying from an upper window. An old cat, palpable as a second-hand fur coat, drowses among the buttercups.

We know when we were born but –

The times of our reprieves are equally random.

Shake it out and look at it again, the flowers, fruit and bright stain of henna, the Russian dolls, the wrinkling chiffon of the flesh, the old songs, the cat, the woman of eighty; the woman of forty, with dyed hair and most of her own teeth, who is *ma semblable, ma soeur*. Who now recedes into the deceptive privacy of a genre picture, a needlewoman, a quilt maker, a middle-aged woman sewing patchwork in a city garden, turning her face vigorously against the rocks and trees of the patient wilderness waiting round us.

From *Burning Your Boats: Collected Short Stories*, published by Vintage.

The Outsider

ISABEL MILLER

D A D D Y   S A I D he couldn't spare the cash right then for plane fare.

I said I'd spend my own.

Lee Ann said it wasn't quite spending my *own* if she and Daddy had to replace it, now was it? She said I keep forgetting I'm only one member of a large family.

I said I don't forget it.

Lee Ann said it seemed to her I'd had just a *bit* more than my share, what with my orthodontist and my contact lenses and not getting a scholarship, and now the shrink, and she would be pretty much in favor of washing her hands of me if I couldn't stay away from my mother, considering who it was that messed me up and made me not study hard enough to get a scholarship, and who made me need the shrink. ('Your therapist,' she calls him.)

'If you like your mother so much, go live with her,' Lee Ann said. 'I wish you would. Let *her* pay for your therapist. She's the one who should. Let her lady friend pay for your therapist, I mean, *excuse* me. I realize she can't, herself. She can only *make* problems, not do anything about them.'

I just kept quiet and hated her and concentrated on having all my hate show.

Daddy said, 'All right, Rebecca, that's enough.'

I was going to run up to my room and slam the door, the way I always did before. But then I remembered I don't *have* a room anymore. It's the nursery for the new baby.

So then I was going to jump on my bike that Mother bought me when I was ten. She said someday I could go hosteling across Europe on it and take it to college. She always gave me everything too soon – before I was ready for it. Who when they're ten needs a black English gear-shift touring bike? But I grew up to it and lots of times I zoomed off into the night on it when I couldn't stand Lee Ann anymore and she couldn't stand me, and Daddy let me do it because he had to keep on the good side of Lee Ann. He runs this whole marriage scared, afraid to fail again. And Lee Ann wouldn't be nice about everything the way Mother was. Lee Ann would clean him out, and he knows it.

But my bike was up at school. So I took Emily's out of the garage. I knew she wouldn't mind. She likes me. She really does. It's crazy. All I've ever done since we were little is boss her around and tease her and kick her out of games, but she really likes me. She's spineless. She's a real goody-goody Pollyanna type, and she's got 20/20 eyes, the whole bit. She's never had anything but As in school, she's a natural for a Presidential Merit Award, she's always cleaning and helping and being sweet to people and making everybody think she's beautiful and wonderful. She won't cost a cent dentally or mentally or educationally, and she's really crazy about me. She should be. I really make her look good. She just makes me sick. She got along with Mother, and now she gets along with Lee Ann, and she's nice to all the little kids, and I knew she wouldn't mind a bit if I took her bike.

I was just pushing it down the driveway when Lee Ann came out on the porch and asked whose bike *is* that? She was going to explain again about respect for property, so I just threw my leg over and took off. I felt, I think, a lot the way Mother used to when she backed her car out and roared away. I just wanted to go and go, and get real tired.

I felt so *lonesome*, because Daddy didn't dare to be on my side anymore and always stuck up for Lee Ann, even when she was *saying* nasty things and I was merely *looking* nasty, and because Mothery may be fun and interesting, but Lee Ann's right – Mother really can't take care of anybody and I couldn't have a room of my own if I went there either. She's not making any money anymore. The stuff she writes since the divorce nobody will publish. She just *deliberately* writes things she knows no one will publish, and keeps house for Vera and Vera supports her and they're Lesbians in Greenwich Village. And that's what the shrink and I talk about – and also if I am too, and we think probably not, because I truly enjoy boys a lot but on the other hand I could be kidding myself. So Lee Ann's right – Mother, through me, is costing Lee Ann and Daddy a lot of money, but also Mother earned an awful lot when she was writing what people liked and one of her books was even a movie, and when she and Vera went away, all Mother took was her filing cabinet and some books. She didn't even take her car. Vera had one.

So I was riding Emily's bike as fast as I could, heading nowhere special. The starlings were cawing away. Early evening. Pretty soon there'd be fireflies, and fireflies always make me feel so awful unless I'm with somebody I really love a lot. I'd missed the sunset, or the best of it, trying to get plane fare to Mother. There's this hill west of town I like to climb every night to watch the sunset over the lake. It sounds corny, but practically every night, unless I had play rehearsal, or I had to put some last-minute touches on the school paper, I used to climb up that hill and watch the sunset until the evening star came out and then I'd wish on the evening star and go home. I wished for love. I told Mother about it last summer, and she said the evening star is usually Venus, and love is exactly what Venus should be prayed to for.

I was wondering whether to try for the last of the sunset when I heard bike wheels, and it was Daddy, on *Rosemary's* bike. Like Lee Ann said, we're a big family. Our garage looks like a bike factory. The cars have to stay out in the weather.

Daddy handed me a flashlight and I put it into the clip and we rode along not looking at each other. I was afraid he'd look silly and try to make me laugh, him with his long legs on a little girl's bike with the seat way low. I used to think he was so amusing. So wonderful and silly. Or else he'd try to get into a heart-to-heart talk, starting, 'How are you, Becky?' I just hate it

when he says, in that awful *earnest* way, 'How are you, Becky?'
He used to say that a lot after Mother went away, before he got
all wrapped up in Lee Ann.

But he didn't say anything and we just rode along, and all of
a sudden I knew he was missing Mother too.

I'm very good at knowing what people are thinking. Like one
time, Mother was standing at the sink looking out the window,
and I just knew, and I said, 'What are you admiring?' And actually
she had no real expression at all. She said, 'Just daydreaming,'
but I ran to another window and looked out and saw a pretty
lady in a purple dress walking along with her butt kind of gently
jiggling. I was about five then. I never forget anything, either,
and that was one of the things I put together to figure out about
Mother and Vera. Also a little while after Vera started coming
around our house, I dreamed that Mother and Daddy got
divorced. I tell you I *know* things. All except what *I* am and
what I'm supposed to do and what's going to happen to me.

So I knew Daddy was missing Mother, and feeling bad because
there wasn't one single person he could admit it to. Grownups
don't seem to have any friends. I mean, people they really talk
with. I don't see how they stand it, keeping everything inside, and
just talking about the ballgame or the garden. To me, friendship is
practically the most important thing, and I have quite a few very
good friends except they all go to Europe or somewhere every
summer. But I know all their secrets and they know mine. They
know all about Mother and Vera, and which boys I've let do it,
and I know all about who's got a grandmother in a mental
hospital, and whose very bigshot father tried to murder his whole
family, and whose mother is drunk every afternoon, and who's
bedding down with who. Which boys love boys, which girls love
girls. I mean, our whole group, everybody knows everything like
that. And it all seems kind of natural and human, and you don't
look down on anybody and it's all easy.

But grownups. I really have to think they don't know very
much about life. I know that sounds like what kids always think,
but it's really true. And how can they know anything, when they

never really tell each other anything and never read anything? Like, Daddy reads *Time* and his professional journals, and the newspaper. Lee Ann reads *Cosmopolitan* and stuff like that – because Daddy didn't want another intellectual woman, that's for sure – so they thought if I had to be yelled at to clean my room or do my homework, they had some huge awful problem like nobody ever had in the world before.

Mother left the house just crammed with wonderful books, but they're all in boxes in the basement now, getting mildewy. I've spent quite a lot of time down there reading them. Emily's getting so she wants to, too, but I sock her and won't let her. I tell her Mother specifically stated that Emily was not to use these books. I'm so mean to Emily and she keeps liking me. She's crazy. But I don't see why Emily or *anybody* else should, for instance, see Mother's poetry books – Edna St Vincent Millay and Elinor Wylie and all – and see what she underlined and the little remarks she wrote in the margins when she was younger than I am now. When I see the young dumb things she used to say, I feel like I have to protect her.

And anyway, Emily gets along with Lee Ann. She doesn't have a right to Mother, while she's getting along with Lee Ann.

Well, I knew Daddy was missing Mother, and wanting to talk about her. I knew he wouldn't bring her up, and I almost felt sorry enough for him to bring her up myself. It's really pitiful, how even when I got back from seeing Mother last summer he didn't ask me anything about her, and how bored and wrapped up in his newspaper or TV he tried to act if I said anything about her, with his ears practically in points and practically sending out beeps.

I rode along wondering if I was madder or sorrier at him. He really did let me down, whenever it was between me and Lee Ann, even though back when it was me and Mother fighting he was always on my side. Did he have a right to hear about Mother, when he never took her side when he had her here? I thought this way and that way, and finally I decided to say, 'Mother's hair's getting real gray,' and said it.

He just stopped pedaling and when I turned to see where he was, he was turning around and heading home with his knees sticking out like oars. I didn't mean to hit him that hard.

I thought I might follow, but the same reason I had to go out was still in force, and made it so I couldn't go back. I didn't live there anymore. The trouble was, I didn't live anyplace else either.

So I decided I'd go see Tammy and stay the night with her, even though her mother's real afraid Tammy's a Lesbian and makes everybody sleep apart and it wouldn't be any fun. Tammy was the only girlfriend I had that wasn't away for the summer. Otherwise I wouldn't have gone there, because her mother's right, Tammy is a Lesbian about me. Last spring I kissed her, and I didn't get much out of it, but Tammy fell in love with me.

Like I knew she would be, Tammy was real glad to see me in a sappy foolish way, like no poise at all and this little kiddish nervous giggle, and she's my age, she's seventeen, there's no excuse for that. I don't mean I don't like her. I like her a lot. Just not the way she wishes I did.

And it felt good to be welcomed somewhere, except by her mother, who never let us out of her sight except to go to the bathroom once. While she was gone I gave Tammy a quick kiss with some tongue-tip, because it was such fun to see her blush. She has this very thin pink skin. Add a blush to that, and it's like she's bleeding.

I wrote to Mother about kissing Tammy, thinking she might be pleased, but she gave me hell, a little, and told me not to mess around with sincere people until I felt sincere myself. I could see whose side she was on in *that*. Tammy always said, even before she knew why, that she wished she had my mother instead of her own. And I think Mother would have been glad right then to have Tammy instead of me as her daughter.

From A *Dooryard Full of Flowers*, published by The Women's Press.

139

In the Deep Heart's Core

BECKY BIRTHA

I

THOSE PLACES up the coast had wonderful names. Point Reyes. Mendocino. Inverness. That last one always made Sahara think of the place in the Yeats poem, The Lake Isle of Innisfree:

I will arise and go now, and go to Innisfree.

Sahara came to this part of the country for the first time when she first struck out on her own. Twenty years have passed since then, and now she has returned. She has come back to a particular place, this time. But that first time, twenty years ago, she traveled up and down this road for no better reason than that she liked the sound of the names.

At the end of one of those long ago days, she had stood by a roadside, hitchhiking. She'd had no luck the past half hour, and had walked maybe two or three miles already along the road, turning to stretch her arm out straight every time a car passed. There was gritty sand in her socks. Sand had worked its way under her kerchief and settled in her scalp, among the thick, coarse crinkles of her hair. Sand clung beneath her nails and lined the pockets of the faded smock she wore over her patched up blue jeans. She stood with her feet planted far apart, and was glad of her big-boned frame, taking up its space, glad of her height – her size letting them know she could take care of herself. Being outdoors all summer long had bronzed her face from tan to copper brown, and she was glad of it, the earth color distinct to everyone who passed, glad of who she was.

Night was coming. The sun slanted red, sinking over the ocean side of the road. Watching it, she had seen the foot path that led off down the bank. She had crossed the road and followed it. She didn't know that there was another way in, a steep rutted drive a little ways up the highway. She had been surprised to find the space the path led her to scattered with colorful cars and vans.

When she found herself was not on the beach she had expected, but on an enormous wide plateau, a grassy place that was open and expansive, yet sheltered and hidden. It was walled on one side by the sandy banks that led up to the road. She had walked through the long grass, across to the other edge of the open field, and found that the land ended abruptly in a sudden drop down a sheer cliff to the sounding ocean hundreds of yards below. She stood at the edge; the wind whipped through her, and she could see far out to sea. Later, someone told her it was as far west as you could go. The Headlands, she found out they called it.

It was a place where people gathered – folk traveling up and down the coast. Some of them were on holiday – summer gypsies who'd return to some snug town place in a week or a month. Others, in ancient khaki garb and run-down boots, looked as though they had been on the road all their lives. And there were a few who, like Sahara, seemed to be just finding a place from which to begin. They had come in beat-up cars or housecars – pickup trucks with handmade houses perched on their beds – in battered, rusted-out vans and panel trucks, or brightly painted ones. Some, like her, had come walking or hitchhiking, everything they still cared about owning on their backs. They would stay a night, a week, make friends, make love, make decisions about their lives, move on.

Now, twenty years later, Sahara is one of those who has driven here – in a battered blue van. She is not sure why she is back on the road. Or for how long. She did not give notice at the school where she has worked for the past five years. But when she closed up her classroom in June, packing the supplies away, scrubbing the chairs and cots, taking down the posters and bulletin boards, she felt that it was the last time. She couldn't keep on, year after year, loving a whole new class of children, then letting them go.

When she set out in her van at the start of this summer, it seemed there was something drawing her back to this place she had found quite by accident so long ago. It seemed there was something calling her here, some voice that did not stop. Was it the ocean, sounding night and day against the cliffs down below the Headlands, the ocean calling to her? She doesn't know – only knows that if she stays, time will tell why she has come back.

She has been here for three nights and three days now, and has found that twenty years have not changed the place much. Traveling people have not forgotten it. At night someone will build a fire and people will share whatever they have. It is nearly night now. Sahara has taken the largest pot, and gone across the road for water.

Down the road, she first sees the girl, standing where a car has just left her off. The girl faces the traffic that doesn't come, her boots planted far apart. The sun is in her eyes, but she doesn't shade them, and she doesn't take the pack off her back and let it down to rest in the sand by the side of the road. She hasn't a sign with a destination on it. But she does have a map – draws it out of her back pocket and opens it out. She turns to look back up the road and then moves her finger across the map. She folds it to a different square, studies it a little longer, and shoves it into the back pocket of the brown corduroys.

A moment later, she notices the path sloping down the bank between the scrubby bushes, just across the road. Sahara watches the way she hitches up the pack a bit, then looks up and down the road. And Sahara knows the girl is imagining a soft beach to sleep on tonight, high above the level of the tide, just as Sahara did when she first came to this place, very young, on foot, and alone.

Sahara would have been called a girl then, too. Now there is ash gray in the short hair that is tied up beneath her fringed kerchief. Under the spigot, the water splashes over a network of tiny wrinkles on her hands. And when she lifts the pot, the veins stand out on the back of her hand and arm. Her skirt sweeps the grasses as she follows, in long, even strides, down the path where the girl disappeared.

Already, there is a ring of faces around the firelight. Whatever they have brought, they will share. Some nights there is little. Wild peas someone has gathered along the road, thrown into the stew. Abalone or a little fish. Wild berries. Other nights, people stopping have brought food, and there is plenty.

This is one of the nights of plenty. There's meat, and someone has brought fresh sourdough bread.

Two long-haired children tag each other in and out of the firelight, until the smell from the big pot finally draws them in and settles them still.

The girl from the roadside has found her way to the gathering and is standing at the back of the circle. Someone calls out to her, 'Come on over by the fire. Pull up a chair.'

The girl shows a brief flicker of a smile, and moves in next to Sahara. The sudden closeness of her changes something in the air, draws Sahara to an alertness, an awareness that feels like wakefulness of a part of her that has been asleep. She feels, too, as if she's wise to something the girl doesn't yet know – having watched her on the road, maybe. She feels there is a reason the girl has chosen her, out of the circle, to sit beside – some reason the girl herself is not conscious of. She turns to speak. The girl's eyes are wary.

'I'm Sahara,' Sahara says. And then, 'If you've got a cup or a bowl or something, you might want to get it out.'

A big woman in overalls with a blue star tattooed on her arm is ladling out the stew. She holds up a wooden bowl and someone says, 'Over here,' and the bowl is passed that way. When she gets to the girl's blue and white enameled cup, someone says, 'It's his,' jerking a thumb over beside Sahara.

The girl shakes the hair out of her eyes and reaches to take the cup. 'Hers,' she says with half a smile on her lips. But she says it so softly that only Sahara hears it.

To Sahara, it's clear that the girl is a womanchild, nearly a woman. It would have been, even in this gathering darkness, even if Sahara had not seen her on the road. Perhaps her clothes are deceiving. Besides the boots and corduroys, she is wearing a denim jacket with the sleeves cut off. There is nothing on her arms, and there seems to be nothing beneath the jacket. She hasn't any breasts.

But her face is a woman's face. The brown eyes are wide and uncertain, and her mouth, even just smiling halfway, changes the whole look into something so far from harshness you know she is somebody's daughter. Beneath the locks of short brown hair, Sahara can see tiny drops of silver in her earlobes. The girl's skin is tanned. Her face makes Sahara think of a locket – a heart-shaped locket shut tight on a secret.

She knows she has never seen this person before, and yet she can feel herself straining to place her, to figure out who she is. She watches the girl, and the girl watches silently while the others talk.

'I'm thinking about going up around the Russian River, see if there's any work in the lumber business.'

'I don't know. Up in Oregon, where I come from, people been laid off that worked there thirty years.'

A baby wakes and starts to cry. A woman reaches to take it from its father, holds it in the crook of her arm and lifts up her sweater on one side.

Sahara looks away. It hurts her to watch that – something she will never have now.

'Brought the whole family this time, huh?' Someone says to the father with a grin.

'Oh, yeah. Even brought the kitchen sink. We live in that yellow pickup over there. That little fella's never lived in a house, and I hope he never will.'

Sahara watches the girl next to her as her eyes follow the

man's finger, over to the cabin that is perched on the back of the pickup, with its gabled roof and stained glass windows and domed skylight. The girl's eyes widen, and she keeps on looking at it for a long time.

The talk eddies and swirls around them. The fire burns lower. Some people depart for the café in the town, a few miles away. And the children are put to bed. The girl's backpack would make a fine backrest or pillow, but she sits bolt upright, with her back straight. Her legs are crossed, and every part of her is stiffly still. Only her fingers never stop moving, itching, twisting around one another, clasping and unclasping, opening and closing. She stares into the fire. The firelight flickers and leaps in her womanchild's face, in her wide eyes.

Sahara knows she must be the one to begin. In her low voice, she phrases one of the two age-old questions of the road. 'Where you from?'

The girl startles from the trance of the fire, and turns to look at her. In the moment that it takes, Sahara imagines herself as this girl must see her. Old. To someone as young as her, Sahara's near forty years will seem much older than they seem to Sahara. The girl won't see the gray that salts her hair. It's covered with the bright gold kerchief, tied like an Arab headdress, hanging down her neck and back. But even in the firelight, she'll see the lines in Sahara's face, the crow's-feet at the corners of her eyes, and likely the hairs on her chin. She will see old. And black. An old black woman in dowdy clothes from a second-hand store, with a gaudy headrag wrapped around her head. She won't see who Sahara really is.

The girl has turned back to stare at the fire, after answering the question with just one word. 'Oakland.'

Sahara watches her a minute more. It is the girl's fingers that won't be still in her lap, that finally make her go on and ask the other question.

'Where you headed?'

She sighs a long sigh, and says, 'Just traveling.' But she draws up one knee to lean against and turns to Sahara.

'Me, too,' Sahara says, smiling. 'Just traveling, this time. You been on the road long?'

The girl shakes her head from side to side. 'I just left home. This morning.'

'No kidding? This morning? For the first time?'

'Yeah. Well, I ran away a couple of times before. But I was just a kid. This is different. This time I won't go back there. Ever!'

'What happened?' As soon as she's said it, she knows it's wrong. And the girl, who'd turned to face her, now jerks her gaze away, back to the fire.

'It was just time for me to leave, that's all. It wasn't really my home anyway. It was my grandparents' place. And it was time for me to get out, that's all.' Now she has drawn up the other knee, her arms wrapped tight around, so that her shape is a hard, stiff triangle.

'I guess that time comes for everybody,' Sahara says. 'Everybody who's ever going to be her own person.' She stares into the fire, remembering how it was. 'I left home when I was eighteen. My mother thought the world of me, and tried to give me everything, but it wasn't enough for me. I had to have something of my own.' She had always meant to go back and set things right with her mother, years later when she would be an equal, married, with children of her own, when the things they had quarrelled over wouldn't matter any more. She'd always thought there'd be plenty of time for that and then, one summer, when Sahara was halfway around the world, her mother had suddenly died. . . .

'I went on the road, too,' she tells the girl beside her. 'That was all I wanted to do. Hitchhike cross-country. Get out to California. Didn't know the first thing about how to do it. I mean, I didn't even know how to read a road map right to get out of my home town. First time a tractor trailer ever stopped for me, I didn't know how to climb up there. I didn't know some pretty basic safety stuff I ought to've known either. Like to check the locks on the doors of the car before you get in, make sure you can get out.' She's eyeing the girl's profile, hoping she's listening, wishing she'd ask what else. There's so much Sahara knows now that would have made things easier, if someone had told her. 'Or even,' she says, 'to always go to a woman if you get in trouble and need some kind of help. Don't ever depend on a man.' She waits, but the girl doesn't answer, doesn't ask. And Sahara knows how scared she is.

People are returning from the town. Somewhere, someone picks up a guitar, and a quiet song spills out of the nearby darkness. Sahara stands; her skirt falls in billows to the ground. She stretches, reaching her hands out for one last feel of the fire's warmth, then moves away, to do the things she needs to do for the night.

She collects her sleeping bag from the battered blue van and comes back by way of the fire, crouching for a second beside the girl. 'You got a sleeping bag? Or blankets or anything?'

'Huh? Oh, yeah. A sleeping bag.'

'It's a good night for sleeping out,' Sahara says. 'I've got an old van here, but I only use it when it rains.' She nods her head over toward the far side of this grassy place, away from the road. 'I always like to sleep out there, on the Headlands. In the morning when you wake up, you can look right out over the ocean.'

'I think I'll just stay here awhile longer,' the girl says.

'Got a lot on your mind to think about, huh?'

'Yeah,' she says. 'Yeah, I guess so.'

'Well, if it helps your thinking any to talk, come over and talk to me. I'll be awake a bit longer. And I wake up easy, too. I don't mind – if something's troubling you.' She smiles at the girl, trying to let her know that she wants to be a friend.

'Thanks,' the girl says. And smiles back – a self-conscious smile, but a whole one, this time. It makes Sahara feel as if a door has suddenly swung wide open in this night, a door into a bright, new place that has never been entered.

The wind is high, blowing shreds and shards of gray clouds across a three-quarter moon. Sahara places her sleeping bag with the head facing the bluffs. She turns her shoes upside down and makes a pillow, under the sleeping bag, of the sweater she has taken off. Then she lies still in her bag, on her back, and lets the memories come flooding in. It is the children that she is always remembering, all the children who have passed through her life.

II

The first time Sahara went to sleep in a house where she was alone with children, she had a hard time sleeping. In her head she went over in detail the whole layout of the house, with its abundance of doors and halls and private baths. She did not know it as well as she should, and wondered if she could really find her way if there were a fire and she was half asleep.

The Weatherbys had not bothered to question how she might deal with emergencies, or even ask what her experience had been. They had looked at her and not seen a teenager who had never done anything like this before. They had seen, in her dark face and her tall, womanly frame, only generations of cooks and 'help', nursemaids and nannies.... The interview with Mrs Weatherby hadn't even taken fifteen minutes. The woman was so overjoyed at finding someone on such short notice, so relieved that she would not have to cancel the week in the Bahamas after all, that she had explained all this in much greater detail than she explained about Heather's temper tantrums or Bradley's asthma.

In the stuffy little spare room, Sahara worried until she couldn't keep her eyes open any longer. Three hours later she was wide awake, as though a voice had called her. Down the long hall, there was only silence, but she threw on her robe and padded in her bare feet to the rooms where the children slept.

Peter Weatherby was hunched in the middle of his bed with the covers pulled over his head. He was crying. Sahara sat by his side and rubbed his back in wide, slow circles. She did not want to talk or sing, afraid she might wake the others. So, very softly, she recited poems to him – 'The Owl and the Pussycat,' 'Wynken, Blynken and Nod,' 'Little Brown Baby' – all the ones that her own mother had read to her, over and over again. Her hand kept stroking the warm dampness of his soft pajamas, circling in the rhythm of the verses – until he slept.

Still she sat there, a long time after, watching the mound of his small body rise and fall in gentle regularity. He had cried. And she, at the other end of the hall, the other end of the house, had not heard, but had known. He had cried and she had put him back to sleep. It was as if she had passed through some ritual, some initiation. . . .

In the night, there are only quiet noises, the ocean at the foot of the cliffs, and the dry grasses rustling. The wind is restless still, whirrs in Sahara's ears and washes her bare face cold and clean. Overhead, most of the clouds have blown off and stars are out.

The ancient rhyme comes into her head. 'Starlight, starbright, first star I see tonight . . .' She has always made the same wish, over and over, on every star and wishbone, every milkweed seed caught and dandelion blown away, on all the birthday candles. Whenever she heard the words 'heart's desire,' she thought of a child.

She never wanted a man. And she chose a way of life – without men – in which children did not easily appear. Sometimes it seems she has spent her whole life finding ways to get close to other people's children.

The child who did not know how to play was a little girl, a Puertorriqueña. Her name was Elizabeth Maldonado. She was three. Elizabeth's mother came into Sahara's classroom holding her small daughter's hand and gazed around the colorful playroom. She spoke to Sahara in a voice barely loud enough to hear. '*Mi hija, mi Elizabeth – no sabe jugar*. She is not like my other children. She does not play. *Es la única cosa* – that is the one thing I care about . . . maybe . . . you can teach her?'

In the playroom the children clustered around the sandbox that stood on tall legs by the window. They patted up mountains and highways, scooped out tunnels and lakes. Their high-pitched voices bargained and traded, cried for a turn with the dump truck, shrieked with delight.

Elizabeth stood in the center of the room, a crumpled tissue in one hand, a tiny doll house figure in the other. Her slender body swaying in the short cotton dress, she rocked rhythmically heels to toes, toes to heels. There was a whisper of a smile on her face; her eyes were far away.

When Sahara got closer, she could hear her humming – a toneless tune that never began or ended, just went on and on. Sahara stooped to the little girl's level and lightly put an arm around her shoulders, smiling into her eyes. 'What's that you have in your hand, Elizabeth? *¿Qué tienes en la mano? Ah – una muñeca.* Can you say that? *Muñeca. ¿Es tuyo?*'

On the playground those first weeks of fall, the other children would come tumbling over to her, short brown and tan and pale legs pumping, untied sneakers and soft plastic sandals pounding across the asphalt. 'Teacher!' '*Maestra!*' 'Miss Sahara!' 'Elizabeth doesn't want a turn to ride.' 'Can I have Elizabeth's turn, Miss Sahara? Please?'

'Oh, no. Elizabeth *needs* her turn. Where is she? *Vente, Elizabeth. Ven acá.*' Taking her by the hand, she led her to the tricycle, while the little girl lagged back and shook her head. 'Come on go for a ride. We'll go slow – *muy suave.*'

Come, Elizabeth. I'll climb the sliding board with you. I'll touch the sticky paste first. We'll pat the rabbit together . . .

In January, Franklin crossed the playroom, his chestnut round face more pleased than angry. 'Hey, you know what, Miss Sahara? Elizabeth talked to me. She said, "You go away!"'

Another day, Manuela came crying. 'Elizabeth took the baby's bottle. I had it first.' In the playhouse corner, Sahara could see Elizabeth, tangly brown hair curtaining her face, slight figure bent over the carriage, holding the plastic nursing bottle to the baby doll's mouth.

There was an afternoon on the playground again, nearly the last week of school, and the end of the day. Across the street she could see Mrs Hughes waiting for the light to change, and

Franklin had seen her too, was already collecting his paintings and the wooden airplane he had made. Down the block, Mrs Maldonado came pushing the baby's stroller in front of her.

Sahara looked around for Elizabeth. The little girl was just starting up the ladder of the sliding board. She was always very serious about this, hands clamping the railings, patent leather pumps stepping one rung at a time, her small chin set with determination. Sahara stopped her for a second with her hand on the child's back. 'When you get up to the top, look and see who's coming.'

The child reached the summit. She stood between the high arched railings, a hand on each one, and scanned the horizon. And her tiny face broke into a furious grin. ¡Mami! ¡Mami! ¡Mira, Mami!

She swept down the shining length of the slide, landing on her feet and ran, brown hair flying, ran laughing across the entire playground, out the open gate, and into her mother's arms.

Sahara will never forget the image of that little girl, arms open, laughing and running – away from her. She will not forget any of them, though years have passed, and they are scattered in different cities all across the country. Quiet nights in open places, the boundaries are unguarded, and they come back to her. Peter and Elizabeth and so many others. Like Joy.

Sahara lived with Joy, Joy's mother Janet, four other women and two other children in a big sprawling old house in the heart of the city, maybe ten years ago, now. Joy was another child who couldn't play. Tamika and Nicholas would be racing up and down the stairs after school, calling out to each other and shouting. 'I can't find my skate key!' 'Hey, will you hold the door while I get my bike out?' 'Wait up! Wait for me!'

Joy's delicate dark fingers closed only with straining effort around a crayon or pencil, and the pictures came out a snarl of faintly marked scribbles. Bikes and skates, even scissors and puzzles were impossible.

Tamika and Nicholas ran in and out – for a piece of chalk, a glass of water – the door screen banging behind them. Sahara sat on the couch with Joy in her lap, the soft pile of Joy's short hair against her cheek, and read picture book after picture book. 'And when he came to the place where the wild things are they roared their terrible roars . . .'

'And gna-a-ashed their ter-ri-ble tee-e-eeth . . .,' Joy's small voice drawled, forcing out the syllables one by one with effort. The words came out distorted, but she had them all memorized. After living with her for a month, Sahara could understand almost everything Joy said. It was like listening to words slowed down on a tape recorder that she could speed up in her head. Or like learning to decipher someone's handwriting. 'And ro-o-olled their ter-ri-ble eye-s . . .'

'And showed their terrible claws.' Outside, she could hear Tamika and her girlfriends.

'That ain't the way you draw a hopscotch, girl. Onesies posed to be all by itself.' 'I'm first, when she get finished.' 'Nu-uh! I already said it.'

Tamika and Nicholas were only a year and two years older than Joy. But they didn't play with her. Sahara had heard one of Tamika's friends asking once, just outside the window, 'How come your sister still has to be in a stroller?' And Tamika declaring hotly, 'That's not my sister!'

Nicholas and Tamika had quickly made friends with each other and made their own friends in the neighbourhood. Their friends lived with mothers and fathers, or mothers and brothers and sisters, or even with grandmothers, but not with multi-ethnic collections of odd assorted women who weren't related to them or to each other. Their friends were never invited in, by either Tamika or Nicholas.

' . . . And into the night of his very own room where he found his supper waiting for him and it was still hot.' She closed *Where the Wild Things Are* and slapped it down on the pile on the floor below them, spilled Joy onto the couch and stood up. 'That's it.

I'm not reading any more stories. Know what we're gonna do now?'

'Wha-a-at?'

'We're gonna sail away. To where the wild things are.'

A table turned upside down was their boat, the broom and mop were oars. Joy steadied the sail and kept a sharp look out for islands on the horizon. Sahara rowed and sang 'Heave Away Santyanna' and 'The Sloop John B.' They caught fish with one of Joy's long shoelaces. And then Joy dropped the sail, her palms patting the upturned underside of the table beneath her. Her eyes were pools of dismay. 'O-oh no-o.'

'What is it? What's the matter?' Sahara was instantly alert, the play forgotten.

'It's we-et.'

Sahara began to pat the floor too, feeling anxiously around Joy's bottom. Everything was absolutely dry. Joy heaved out a guffaw of laughter at Sahara's antics and finished triumphantly, 'I think we ss-pru-ung a lee-e-eak.'

They were busy bailing out when Nicholas came in, and didn't notice him until he walked through the ocean and right up to the side of the boat and said, 'Hey what are you doing? How come you turned over the table?'

'This isn't a table,' Sahara corrected.

Joy grinned and said, 'If you do-on't sstart sss-wim-ming you're go-ing to dro-o-own.'

'Can I play?' Nicholas asked.

Sahara nearly answered, but Joy cut her off. 'I kno-o-ow.' Her voice was loud and sure. 'He can be one of the wi-i-ild things.'

Whatever became of them? Joy would be fifteen or sixteen now, Nicholas maybe eighteen. But the house had broken up at the end of the first year. Eventually, she had lost touch with all of them.

When Sahara sleeps, she dreams of children. Babies and children – they come to her in dreams every night. Each is distinct and different from any other. Each has her own voice, his own shape, her own face like no one else in the world.

III

Something has awakened her on this night, just as it did on that first night long ago, knowing that one of the children was awake, and in trouble.

She listens. The wind has died as it always does, along toward morning. The night is absolutely still. Only the tops of the grasses rustle softly. Above her, the clouds have all blown off; the vast blackness is alight with stars, the milky way cutting a wide swath across the center. The girl has brought her sleeping bag and stretched it out on the ground along next to Sahara's.

Sahara sits up and studies the figure beside her. There's a scent of dye and fresh fabric from the sleeping bag – it must have been bought new for this adventure. Its inhabitant lies still, with her face turned away and half covered. Sahara knows she is crying.

She hesitates, torn over whether to allow the girl her space, or to enter it. Where does she belong in this person's life? Does she belong at all? Finally she reaches out and rests a hand for a moment on the girl's shoulder through the thick, quilted material. 'I'm awake,' she says, 'if you want to talk about it.'

The girl doesn't answer at first. Then her voice comes out, scratchy with tears. 'That won't help.'

'Maybe not. Maybe it won't change anything. But if you tell someone, then at least you don't have to carry it all by yourself.' She waits a moment, then goes on. 'You know, that's one of the things I found out is so special about the road – it keeps your secrets for you. You can talk to somebody you just met and tell them anything. After tonight you never have to see me again.' She waits a bit longer, then asks, 'What happened?'

'Nothing,' the girl says.

'I mean back at home – *something* happened.'

'I just had to get out of there, that's all. It wasn't my home, anyway. They never let me forget *that*.'

'Did they . . . did your grandparents throw you out?'

The girl has squirmed to sit up, wiping her face with the heels of her hands. Now she laughs a laugh that is like a handful of stones thrown down on concrete. 'I told him not to bother. The bastard. I told him not to waste his breath. Said I was capable of walking out that door without any help from him. And I did it, too.'

'Something he did made you furious . . .'

'Everything he did drove me crazy! He's always so smug and proud of himself – he can't ever let me forget it for a minute how they took me in and raised me. I'm supposed to be humble and grateful for the rest of my life.' She let another pebble of hard laughter fall. 'That's not giving.'

'Every time I do anything he doesn't like, any little thing, he goes crazy. He said I was going to end up just like her.' She turns, suddenly to seek out Sahara's face in the darkness. 'My mother, I mean. I'm gonna end up another disgrace to the family. Ashamed to come home.' Her eyes hold Sahara's in the quiet, charcoal darkness. 'He calls her a slut. Right to my face. He says that about my mother! He says I'm gonna end up a slut just like her.'

She looks away again, out into the night. Her hands have begun to play with the edge of the quilted fabric, pleating it into harried ruffles, letting it go, taking it up again. 'I didn't even do anything. He won't ever give me a chance to explain. Him and his dirty mind. Just because I was out all night he thinks I was screwing around. I wasn't even with a boy. I was with Marianne Delarosa. Just cause I like to talk to her. We were up talking all night, sitting in her brother's truck.'

She is silent for a few moments, looking out over the distance, out over the Headlands where, far below, the voice of the ocean is suddenly loud, sounding against the rocky wall of the cliff. For a moment, everything about the girl is still; even her fingers lie resting.

'Everybody says my mother ran off with another woman. Some woman she met over in the city that nobody knew. But they won't ever tell me any more than that. They act like it's something I'm not supposed to know. My grandparents won't talk about it at all. Except to point out how I'm turning out just like her.' Her fingers close on a clump of grass beside her and rip the long blades from the ground, tearing them into bits. 'So what if I *am* like her? I'm *supposed* to be like her. She was my mother! She got out of there when she was eighteen and I swore to God I would, too.'

'That must have hurt you a lot,' Sahara says softly. The locket face turns to her; the girl looks surprised that Sahara is still there. 'The way she left you there, I mean,' Sahara says. 'That she got out herself, but she didn't take you – she left you there.'

The girl is brushing sudden fresh tears back from the sides of her face with the heels of her hands. 'It doesn't matter,' she says. 'Because I got out now, too. And I'm going to find her.'

'Your mother?'

'Yeah. That's really why I left – and where I'm going.'

'So she stayed in touch with you?'

'Well, not exactly. We haven't been in touch. But I know she was supposed to have gone up north. Headed for Vancouver. That's what everybody said.'

Sahara looks over to check her face, but the girl is completely serious. She's leaning on one elbow now, her look full of that confidence in herself that doesn't last long past eighteen. 'Vancouver's a big place,' Sahara says softly.

The girl seems not to have heard. 'And I know what she looks like. Everybody says I look just like her.'

'Of course,' Sahara says gently, 'she'd be older now.'

'Of course,' the girl answers, lightly.

'And she must have lived through a lot. I mean, she may not be the person you think she is . . .'

'Then I want to know who she is, now. I want her to know who *I* am.'

And Sahara thinks, no, *you* want to know who you are. You want her to give you that. And she never will, even if you find her. No one can.

'Whoever she is,' the girl says, 'I don't care. She's my mother.

I'm going to find her. I don't care if it takes me the rest of my life.'

Now the girl is lying back, with her arms folded under her head, watching the sky. 'Sure are a lot of stars out here,' she says, and her voice sounds hushed and small against the vast night.

Sahara slips down in her bag and turns on her back to view them, too. 'Sure are. It's funny to think how, down here, they all look close together and pretty much the same. But up there every one is different, and they're millions of miles apart.' She wants to go on: You might as well go wandering off into the sky, little girl, and try to find just one star.

'You know, your mother could be anywhere,' she says, finally. 'She could be camping out right here on this roadside tonight.'

'I never thought of that. I guess she could.' The girl turns that one over in her mind, and says, doubtfully, 'Maybe I should stay here for awhile.' Then she asks, 'Are *you* going to be staying here long?'

'I don't know. I could stay a while longer.' She's thinking, thinking about what happens next, in her life. She listens to the sound of the waves, striking on the rock below, striking and splashing, roaring and repeating. Something like that never-ending sound has called her back here, after all these years, to this place to begin from, begin again.

Twenty years ago, that first time, she sat looking out over these same cliffs another bright, starry night, and a woman sat beside her who seemed old to Sahara then. She was the one who told Sahara what this place was. She said, 'Where we're sitting now is as far west as you can go. This cape is the end of the land, and these Headlands are the end of the cape. Everybody always wants to travel west, but when you get here you have to change directions.'

Sahara lifts up a little to look over at the girl who lies watching the stars. 'I might be going north in another few days,' she tells her. 'It's been a long time since I've been in Vancouver.'

There's some kind of softness, a warmth, that has come stealing up in the windless dark and circled the two of them all the way

Becky Birtha

around. Sahara feels it – something that glows and makes her
happy. She wants to say to the girl: I know who you are. I knew
all along – you were *somebody's* daughter . . . Instead, she asks,
'Do you like Yeats?'

The girl laughs a self-conscious laugh. 'I don't know what they
are.'

And Sahara smiles back in the dark. 'Close your eyes and
listen. It'll help you go to sleep.'

She chants the words softly out into the night between them,
one poem and then another, until the child beside her has fallen
asleep. She goes on to finish, anyway,

'I will arise and go now, for always night and day
I hear lake water lapping with low sounds by the shore;
Where I stand on the roadway, or on the pavements grey,
I hear it in the deep heart's core.'

From *Lovers' Choice*, published by The Women's Press.

Isabel Allende the Chilean novelist, was a journalist for many years. She began to write fiction in 1981. The result was the worldwide bestseller *The House of the Spirits*, which was followed by the equally successful *Of Love and Shadows*, *Eva Luna*, *The Stories of Eva Luna* and *The Infinite Plan*. Her first work of non-fiction, *Paula*, was published in 1995 and is a harrowing chronicle of the death of her daughter. Isabel Allende lives in California.

Margaret Atwood was born in Ottawa in 1939, and grew up in northern Quebec and Ontario, and in Toronto. She has lived in many other cities, including Boston, Vancouver, Edmonton, Montreal, Berlin, Edinburgh and London, and has travelled extensively. She has published over twenty books, including novels, poetry and literary criticism. She lives in Toronto with novelist Graeme Gibson and their daughter Jess.

Toni Cade Bambara was born and brought up in Harlem, New York. She is the bestselling author of *Deep Sightings and Rescue Missions: Fiction, Essays and Conversations* (The Women's Press, 1997), edited and introduced by Toni Morrison; two short story collections, *Gorilla My Love* (The Women's Press, 1984) and *The Sea Birds Are Still Alive* (The Women's Press, 1984); and a novel, *The Salt Eaters* (The Women's Press, 1982). Toni Cade Bambara died on 9 December 1995.

Becky Birtha has published two collections of short stories: *For Nights Like This One: Stories of Loving Women* and *Lovers' Choice*

(The Women's Press, 1988). Her stories and poetry have appeared in a number of literary and feminist journals. She currently lives in Philadelphia, where she is working on a novel.

Bonnie Burnard is a writer, editor and reviewer whose work has been widely anthologised and dramatised. She won the Commonwealth Best First Book Award for *Women of Influence* (The Women's Press, 1993) and has also won several Saskatchewan Writers' Guild Awards. *Casino and Other Stories* was shortlisted for the prestigious Giller Prize for Fiction. She was the 1995 recipient of the coveted Marian Engel Award, joining an esteemed group of Canadian women writers which includes Alice Munro, Carol Shields and Jane Urquhart. She has given readings throughout Canada, the USA, England, Europe, South Africa and Australia. Bonnie Burnard lives in Ontario, Canada.

Angela Carter was born in 1940. She read English at Bristol University, and from 1976 to 1978 was fellow in Creative Writing at Sheffield University. She lived in Japan, the United States and Australia. Her first novel, *Shadow Dance*, was published in 1965, followed by *The Magic Toyshop* (1967, John Llewellyn Rhys Prize), *Several Perceptions* (1968, Somerset Maugham Prize), *Heroes and Villains* (1969), *Love* (1971), *The Passion of New Eve* (1977), *Nights at the Circus* (1984, James Tait Black Memorial Prize) and *Wise Children* (1991). Four collections of her short stories have been published: *Fireworks* (1974), *The Bloody Chamber* (1979, Cheltenham Festival of Literature Award), *Black Venus* (1985) and *American Ghosts and Old World Wonders* (1993); they have been collected together as *Burning Your Boats* (1995). She was the author of *The Sadeian Woman: An Exercise in Cultural History* (1979), and two collections of journalism, *Nothing Sacred* (1982) and *Expletives Deleted* (1992). She died in February 1992.

Patricia Grace was born in Wellington, New Zealand, in 1937. She is of Ngati Raukawa, Ngati Toa and Te Ati Awa descent, and is affiliated to Ngati Porou by marriage. She has published four collections of short stories: *Waiariki*, which was the first published collection by a Maori woman, came out in 1975 and was followed by *The Dream Sleepers*, *Electric City* and *The Sky People* (The Women's Press, 1995). She has written children's books, of which *The Kuia and the Spider* won the 1982 New Zealand Children's Picture Book of the year; and novels, including *Potiki* (The Women's Press, 1987), winner of the fiction section of New Zealand Book Awards in 1987, and the Liberaturpreis in Germany in 1994; *Mutuwhenua: The Moon Sleeps* (Livewire Books, The Women's Press, 1988); and *Cousins* (The Women's Press, 1993). Patricia Grace has taught in primary and secondary schools and was the Writing Fellow at Victoria University in Wellington in 1985. She is married with seven children.

Sara Maitland is a writer and theologian. Her first novel, *Daughter of Jerusalem*, won the Somerset Maugham Award in 1979; and since then she has published regularly – most recently *Angel and Me*, a collection of short stories commissioned by BBC Radio 4 (1996). She now lives alone in rural Northamptonshire.

Carol Mara is an Australian writer. Her first book, *Eva's Crossing*, was published in 1993.

Isabel Miller is the author of the cherished classic *Patience and Sarah* (1979), as well as *A Dooryard Full of Flowers* (1994), *The Love of Good Women* (1995) and *Side by Side* (1996), all published by The Women's Press. She died in October 1996.

Michèle Roberts was born in 1949 of a French mother and English father. *A Piece of the Night*, published in 1978, was her début novel, and also the first work of original fiction to be published by The Women's Press. It established Michèle Roberts as a major literary writer, and was followed by *The Visitation* (The Women's Press, 1983). Michèle Roberts is now an established and acclaimed writer of poetry and prose, including her sixth novel, *Daughters of the House*, which was shortlisted for the 1992

Booker Prize and won the WH Smith Literary Award 1993. Her eighth novel, *Impossible Saints*, was published in 1997.

Wajida Tabassum was born in 1935, brought up in Amravati and Hyderabad, and is the author of 27 books of fiction and poetry. Her story, *Hand-me-downs*, which appears in this collection, was written in 1975 and has been translated into all major Indian languages. In 1988 it was made into a television programme and has proved to be one of her most controversial stories. Widely travelled, Wajida Tabassum now lives and works in Bombay.

Kathleen Tyau is a Chinese-Hawaiian woman who grew up in the hills above Pearl Harbor on the Hawaiian island of Oahu. Her writing career began at the age of 13, when one of her stories was published in the *Honolulu Star Bulletin*, for which she was paid one dollar. Tyau left Hawaii to attend college in Oregon, where she received her BA in English. After college, she worked as a handweaver, administrative aide for conservation groups, and legal secretary. She was appointed by the governor to serve on the Oregon Heritage Advisory Council. Her novel *A Little Too Much Is Enough* (The Women's Press, 1996) won the Pacific Northwest Booksellers Association award, and her short stories and essays have been published widely. She lives in Oregon, where she windsurfs and hikes in the Columbia Gorge, grows trees, plays bluegrass music, and continues to weave and write.

Alison Ward was born in Hong Kong, and has kept on the move ever since – living in Kenya, Germany, France and various parts of England. She first studied music, then accountancy, and has written one novel, *The Glass Boat* (1984), and a set of plays for video.

Alice Walker was born in Eatonton, Georgia. She has received many awards, including The Radcliffe Institute medal and a Guggenheim Fellowship. Her hugely popular novel *The Color Purple* (The Women's Press, 1983) won the American Book

Award, plus the Pulitzer Prize for Fiction in 1983, and was subsequently made into an internationally successful film by Steven Spielberg. Alice Walker's novels are *Meridian* (1982), of which CLR James said 'I have not read a novel superior to this'; *The Third Life of Grange Copeland* (The Women's Press, 1985); *The Temple of My Familiar* (The Women's Press, 1989), which appeared in the *New York Times* bestseller list for four months; and *Possessing the Secret of Joy* (1992). Her memoir *The Same River Twice: Honoring the Difficult* was published by The Women's Press in 1996. Alice Walker has also written two collections of short stories: *In Love and Trouble* (The Women's Press, 1984) and *You Can't Keep a Good Woman Down* (The Women's Press, 1982); and three books of essays and memoirs: *In Search of Our Mothers' Gardens: Womanist Prose* (The Women's Press, 1984), *Living by the Word* (The Women's Press, 1988) and *Anything We Love Can Be Saved* (The Women's Press, 1997). Alice Walker has published four books of poetry, all of which have been published by The Women's Press: *Horses Make a Landscape Look More Beautiful* (1985), *Once* (1986), *Good Night, Willie Lee, I'll See You in the Morning* (1987) and *Revolutionary Petunias* (1988). Alice Walker's complete poetry is now collected together in *Her Blue Body Everything We Know: Earthling Poems 1965–1990 Complete* (1991), and her complete short stories appear in *The Complete Stories* (1994), both published by The Women's Press. She is also the co-author, with Pratibha Parmar, of *Warrior Marks* (1993).

The Women's Press is Britain's leading women's publishing house. Established in 1978, we publish high-quality fiction and non-fiction from outstanding women writers worldwide. Our exciting and diverse list includes literary fiction, detective novels, biography and autobiography, health, women's studies, handbooks, literary criticism, psychology and self-help, the arts, our popular Livewire Books series for young women and the bestselling annual *Women Artists Diary* featuring beautiful colour and black-and-white illustrations from the best in contemporary women's art.

If you would like more information about our books or about our mail order book club, please send an A5 sae for our latest catalogue and complete list to:

The Sales Department
The Women's Press Ltd
34 Great Sutton Street
London EC1V 0DX
Tel: 0171 251 3007
Fax: 0171 608 1938